## "Don't ever touch me again," she cried

"If you do, I'll seduce you and tell your girl friend every last detail!"
Even as Meredith said them, the words burned in her brain. Dear God, how could she be so cheap and vulgar! A wave of hot color washed over her cheeks, but she refused to reveal her shame, staring Dane out.

"If you end up in my bed, you'll stay there permanently," he told her. "I'll marry you and tame you!"

"Like hell," she retorted. "You can't force me to do anything."

"There's always Mark," he remarked coolly. "Put one foot out of line, sweet cousin, and you'll lose everything—Mark, the money, the prestige of being Maurice Fowler's granddaughter, this home...the lot!"

*And you, Dane,* Meredith thought, *I'll lose you, too....*

# ROBYN DONALD

## the interloper

*Harlequin Books*

TORONTO • LONDON • LOS ANGELES • AMSTERDAM
SYDNEY • HAMBURG • PARIS • STOCKHOLM • ATHENS • TOKYO

Harlequin Presents edition published July 1981
ISBN 0-373-10441-3

Original hardcover edition published in 1981
by Mills & Boon Limited

# CHAPTER ONE

'WHERE's the sprig?'

Meredith looked up from the over-full plate she was carrying with a smile which made her seem more like a mischievous fifteen-year-old than a staid four-years-older.

'I've left him with a baby-sitter,' she responded, adding with a wry smile, 'I doubt if he'd enjoy this over-much. Two-year-olds are very, very conventional little beings.'

'He's a charmer, just the same.' Like you, the man's eyes intimated, but he had been on the island for a week now and he knew that Meredith Colfax was not interested in even the mildest of flirtations.

'How about coming to join us?' he suggested. 'I know we're a big family, but there's always room for one more.'

Without hesitation she agreed. Don was nice, an Australian with a boisterous sense of humour which hid somewhat surprising sensitivity, and during the week she had been there she had come to know and like his parents as well as the assorted brothers and sisters and cousins who made up their party. Tropical islands were a great forcing house for friendships. Hibiscus Island especially; known throughout the South Pacific as the ideal family resort, it was a small gem on the dry side of the main island of Fiji, palm-shaded, coral-fringed in a sapphire sea.

Left to herself Meredith would have preferred a quieter, less hectically enthusiastic place, but she had needed a place geared to children, and certainly Hibiscus Island resort had been marvellous for Mark, who was now as healthy-looking a little specimen of humanity as any of the delicious little Fijian babies she had seen in her short time in these enchanted islands.

Don's family greeted her with noisy enthusiasm, made room for her at their table and included her in their conversation, not caring in the least that their voices were louder, their laughter more uninhibited than any others in the room.

'Baby asleep?' Mrs Poole asked.

Meredith nodded, grateful that Don's mother had never betrayed by look or word or expression any reservation about befriending a single mother. 'Yes; one of the maids is looking after him, but he won't wake.'

'He's a darling little chap, and I must say this holiday's done him the world of good. He's as brown as a berry. You'll be pleased.'

'Oh, I am.' Meredith's expression clouded as she thought of the thin, cross, pale little scrap who had arrived on the plane from Britain. Last winter had pulled him down dreadfully. With an effort so strong that it was visible she jerked her mind away from all that had happened during last winter. Just as resolutely she avoided thinking of the future. These ten days had been her bonus, a time of peace and recuperation. She was not going to jeopardise them by dwelling on unpleasant things.

So she smiled, unaware that when she did so the piquant triangle of her face blossomed into beauty, and said lightly, 'Hibiscus Island has been good to both of us, but to Mark most of all. A combination of Fijian sun and Fijian spoiling, I think.'

'They certainly love children,' Mrs Poole agreed with some warmth as her gaze swept complacently around the table. 'Even noisy hooligans like my lot, which speaks a lot for the Fijian character, I think. How long are you staying here, Meredith?'

'I leave the island tomorrow.' Which was not the answer to her companion's question. Meredith felt guilty at evading the older woman's well-meant enquiry, and was grateful when Don leaned over and handed her a glass containing what seemed to be her favourite fruit cocktail.

One sip disabused her of that idea. 'What on earth is it?' she asked, wrinkling her nose with distaste.

'A Tequila Sunrise, and you drink it slowly,' he told her, laughing at her expression. 'I know you don't normally drink, but one will be quite harmless, especially after that enormous meal you've just tucked away.'

It was quite true. Gazing at her empty plate with some astonishment, Meredith realised that she had really eaten all of the delicious foods the smiling waitresses had pressed on her. To be sure, most of it had been superb island salads, fish marinated in lime juice and served with coconut cream, onion and tomato, and a nice little steak from the barbecue. She had demolished the lot.

'Much more of this and I'll be as fat as a pig,' she commented.

Don's eyes ran meaningly down her form. 'Room there for a little extra weight,' he said with the cheerful lack of selfconsciousness normal in a boy with several sisters. 'That *sulu* does great things for you; I've not seen one in such muted colours before. I'll bet you didn't get it on the island. The shop here seems to deal in the most primary of primary colours.'

In honour of the occasion Meredith had donned the long oblong of cloth known as a *sulu*, wearing it as her mother had shown her, gathered in at each side and held between her breasts with a knot. It was material she had seen in a small shop in Nadi, the pattern a soft explosion of muted pinks and greens in an abstract design which hinted at the incredibly lush panorama of the tropics.

'No, I didn't get it here,' she answered, taking another cautious sip at her drink.

As she did so her eyes wandered from table to table, gazing at the holidaymakers as they ate beneath the tufted fronds of the coconut palms. Strings of fairy lights lent a glamorous light to the scene but hid the brilliance of the stars in the velvet sky. A small distance away torches flared around the barbecue, casting romantic shadows. Beside that was the pool, carefully chlorinated and vacuumed each morning. It was impossible to see or hear the waves which lapped on the pale coral sands not many yards away, just as it was difficult to see past the conventional glamour of the scene.

Meredith found herself longing for a deserted stretch of beach or a quiet woodland path far away from garish

lights and laughter and electric guitars playing Hawaiian
music. The noise from the Poole clan had become almost deafening; usually she envied them their total
lack of inhibitions, but tonight she felt drowned by
the laughter and teasing and effortless, wearying enthusiasm.

To hide the disloyal trend of her thoughts she directed a
brilliant smile at Don, before continuing her slow scan of
the guests. Mostly they were family groups, but there was
one who was alone, a tall man who sat in the shade of the
bougainvillea arbour. It was strange to see a solitary
diner in this room of family parties. Although he was half
turned away from them Meredith found her glance wan-
dering in his direction; almost she willed him to look at
her. But he continued, oblivious of her interest, to eat his
meal. Then she noticed something else about him, besides
the fact that his shoulders were exceptionally broad and
his tailor exceptionally good. The waiters were treating
him with a kind of deference which was very far removed
from their usual cheerful insouciance. Perhaps he was a
V.I.P., she surmised, someone from a travel firm here to
see if Hibiscus Island should be put on the itinerary of a
package tour. A second glance brought a change of mind.
He looked too arrogantly at ease for that, more like the
owner of the place.

A remark from Mrs Poole recalled her to her place
beside her; somewhat confused by her sudden interest in
the unknown man, she responded, and thereafter deliberately avoided looking in that direction.

After the barbecue there was a *meke*, a concert put on
by the villagers from along the coast. Meredith had been
there with Mark and thought she recognised some of the
ferocious warriors with their faces painted black as men
who had smiled with great charm at the toddler and the
girl with him; certainly they weren't smiling with any sort
of charm now as they acted out a defiance to an imagi-
nary enemy, waving enormous clubs with every appearance of ferocity.

The tourists clapped, took flashlit photographs and listened intently to the beat of the drum, the tapping of

bamboos and the resonant voices of the men joined by the clear true sounds of the women. When, at last, the un-accompanied voices died away after singing Fiji's best-known song, *Isa Lei*, there was a thunderous round of applause before the resident band turned up the amp-lifiers and began to play one of the latest hits.

Sighing for the breaking of the spell, Meredith turned away, intending to slip away to her little *bure* and relieve the baby-sitter from her duties.

'Hey, don't go yet!' Don caught her arm, grinning down at her with some desperation. 'It's your last night, so be like Cinderella and stay up until midnight!'

Fighting down her first impulse to refuse, Meredith found herself relenting. After all, he had been kind to her; the whole family had been sweet in their way. Perhaps she owed him an hour or so of her time without a toddler in tow. And it was fun to dance, fun to forget that she had the responsibility of caring for Mark, to remember that she was nineteen and this was Fiji and that there was a tropical moon above the palms.

As befitted a family resort the band's selection of tunes was nicely balanced between the pops of today and yes-teryear, so that everyone danced. If Don had hoped to keep Meredith exclusively as his partner he was disap-pointed, for she was asked by all of the male members of the party, and then, as the evening drew on and things as-sumed a very informal atmosphere, she danced with sev-eral from other parties there, her blonde tresses belling out above the pale gold of her shoulders, the impressive reserve which made her seem older than her years fading as she responded to the harmless gaiety of the evening with unforced enjoyment.

At last, however, like the Cinderella Don had called her, she gave a remorseful glance at her watch.

'I must go!' she exclaimed, shocked at the swiftness with which the hours had fled.

Don tried to dissuade her, but as she was adamant finally said, 'O.K., I'll walk you back.'

'Goodness, I can find my own way home,' she chaffed, aware that his open admiration of her had developed into attraction, and that he would probably expect a kiss goodnight.

'I know, but that lot by the pool are a bit noisy. I'll see you back.'

It was true; the high spirits of a portion of the crowd outside had degenerated into rowdiness, and with the frankness which was one of her most basic characteristics Meredith owned that she would be grateful for Don's presence beside her when she walked past them.

She said as much, thinking that his kindness perhaps earned him a farewell embrace, then felt ashamed at her cynicism. Trading kisses for protection made her feel cheap, but it seemed prudish to refuse him just because she felt no more than liking for him.

By the pool there was much laughter intermingled with shrieking, and ample evidence that the rowdiness had been fuelled by alcohol. Meredith schooled her expression into a careful blankness as she walked through the group, grateful for Don's presence. She had seen some of the group on the beach and in the dining room, but had spoken to none of them; the sight of them, flushed and unsteady on their feet, made her shiver with revulsion which had a little fear mixed in it. Perhaps, in spite of her lack of expression, her emotions were too strong to be hidden. One of the men looked up as she and Don came towards them, said something which provoked a burst of laughter, then moved so that he was standing directly in their path.

'Why off so soon, kids?' he asked, his glance bold as it roved the contours of Meredith's body. 'Stay and have a little fun with us before you go to bed.'

His grin as he said the last few words left them in no doubt as to his meaning. Swift colour scorched the delicate skin across Meredith's cheekbones, but desperately hoping that Don would keep control of his temper, she answered, 'Sorry, but no, thanks,' and made to step past him.

Exactly what happened then she did not know, but he must have made to touch her and jostled her, whether by design or unintentionally, into the pool. As she felt herself falling she could hear his laughter, raucous on the warm air, and then she was in the water and making for the steps across the other side.

Don was there to meet her. 'You O.K.?' he muttered anxiously as she emerged from the water.

'Yes, I'm fine. What's happened?' for further shrieks and laughter filled the air, and even as she turned there was another splash, followed in quick succession by two more.

'Oh, they've decided that it's a jolly good idea, so now they're all having a go at pushing each other in. Come on, let's get away.'

After hauling her up the steps he hustled her along the path towards the *bures*, his grip on her hand so strong that she winced. He was angry, but more at what he considered his poor showing than at the insult, Meredith decided, some adult wisdom revealing the truth. And knowing just how painful hurt pride is, she endeavoured to ease it for him.

'I'm so glad you kept your temper,' she said breathlessly, half running to keep up with him. 'I was terrified you'd get angry and start a brawl!'

'I should have thumped him,' he muttered, the fierceness of his tones failing to hide the fact that he despised himself.

'Thank heavens you didn't.' She infused delicate scorn into her voice. 'A drunken idiot like that!'

'He insulted you.'

She laughed suddenly at an irony he could not be aware of. 'He couldn't insult me if he tried. People like that only understand their own kind; they have no idea of how people like us tick. Tomorrow he'll wake up with a head like a pumpin with a hammer in it and a sick stomach. That's punishment enough for him.'

'You're a darling,' he said in a suddenly thickened voice, stopping so suddenly that she was completely taken by surprise.

The kiss, when it came, was tentative and gentle, but he took his time about it, only releasing her when footsteps behind them announced that someone else was heading for one of the *bures*.

'Come on,' he said, his voice uncertain now.

'I've made you all wet.'

He laughed suddenly. 'That's the least of my worries. I wish you weren't going, Meredith. At least give me an address where I can write to you.'

Meredith's future was one in which any and every friend would be doubly precious, but she shook her head firmly. 'It's no use, Don. Holiday romances don't extend beyond the holidays, and this hasn't even been a romance, has it?'

'It could have been,' he said, and kissed her again, this time with all of his considerable strength so that she emerged from his embrace gasping and shaken by the passion he had displayed.

The moonlight fell full on her face, illuminating the cat-shaped triangle, the wide grey eyes, the soft fullness of her mouth. The same moonlight shone full into the face of the man who overtook them then, revealing features strong and proud and set in an expression of glacial contempt.

'You're shivering,' Don said anxiously. 'Come on, here's the path to your *bure*. Run, and you'll warm up a bit.'

By the time they had reached the *bure* she had overcome the momentary touch of panic induced by the presence of the dark unknown, for it had been he, she was convinced. Laughing, she begged Don to stop pulling her so hard.

A dim light within revealed the presence of the house-maid, curled up in the armchair with a book and the radio humming softly in Fijian. As she got up Meredith looked directly at her companion.

'Goodnight, Don—and goodbye.'

He hesitated, then said awkwardly, 'O.K. Good luck, Meredith, wherever you're going,' and turned and left her.

'He slept all the time,' the baby-sitter told her as they walked across the *bure* to where the child lay.

'Good. Thank you so much for being here.'

The maid's handsome features were completely transformed by the flashing smile which all Fijians had in common. 'Have a good time?'

'Lovely, thank you.' Rather selfconsciously Meredith bent to smooth a tress of dark hair back from Mark's cheek.

'He looks like you,' the other girl said. 'Much darker, but everything else is just like you—nose, eyes, mouth.' Her smile widened. 'Bigger chin than his mother, but that's a good thing. A man needs a chin to keep his wife in order.'

When she had gone Meredith showered and climbed into her nightgown, too strung up to contemplate going to sleep yet. As she towelled her hair dry she walked up and down in the darkened room, staring through the wide glass sliding door at the moonlit vista of the sea through the palms and bushes which made each *bure* private. Hibiscus Island was beautiful, a jewel set in a jade sea, made a fairyland by corals and fish which were jewels in themselves. For ten days she had used part of the pitiably small legacy left by her mother to stay here, satisfying her conscience by convincing it that she must regain some strength before she met her grandfather.

Grandfather! Why *grand*? she wondered irrelevantly, trying to still the fear which the thought of him aroused. Grand meant fine, splendid. Incredible to think that she had lived for eighteen of her nineteen years totally unaware that she possessed such a relative. In fact, she hadn't known of his existence until three months ago when her mother, drawn with the pain of the illness which would eventually claim her life, had told her.

He was Maurice Fowler, an autocrat who lived in splendour in Fiji, running the business which spread like tentacles through the South Pacific from a magnificent mansion on the side of a hill above Lautoka, the second biggest town in Fiji.

'It's on the dry side of the main island,' her mother told her, showing her a map of the group of islands which comprised the country of Fiji. 'They grow sugar cane there, acres and acres of it. A funny little train goes puffing through the fields of cane, carrying it to the mill at

Lautoka. And the flowers—ah, Meredith, the flowers are like Paradise.'

She had fallen silent then, smiling in remembrance, but after a few minutes had resumed, telling Meredith an old sad story of a repressed daughter who had run away to marry the man she loved, only to have him desert her after the birth of their first child.

Meredith could understand that runaway match. She too had felt the charm of her father when he had reappeared, not particularly repentant but so full of life and gaiety that both wife and daughter had forgiven him the empty years. The most tangible result of his return to his wife was the child who was now sleeping so peacefully in the bed behind her; about six months after Mark's birth his father had gone sailing for the weekend with friends, a weekend when a storm had blown in from the Atlantic creating such havoc and tragedy that the death of one man as he rescued the small daughter of his hosts had gone almost unnoticed and unremarked.

But his death had taken the will to live from Dinah Colfax and when illness came she had no reserves of strength left to fight it.

'I'm tired,' she said quietly, so quietly. 'And I'm defeated, darling. But your grandfather won't let you starve. He's a hard man and he's never forgiven me for disobeying him, but he has a strong sense of family honour, and it's been his money which has kept us solvent all these years. He'll look after you and Mark.'

Mark was the sort of child who would sleep through an earthquake, so Meredith's snort of disgust now didn't even make him stir.

But the memory of the letter from her grandfather's lawyer was still too raw and painful for her to be able to think calmly about it. Running her fingers through her rapidly drying hair, she paced across to the small fridge, poured herself a glass of iced water, and sat down in the chair so recently vacated by the baby-sitter.

Apparently Maurice Fowler was prepared to undertake the support of his granddaughter and grandson only if they came out to Fiji and remained in his guardianship until they were twenty.

It was no hardship for Meredith to leave her job at the bank, but the thought of poor little Mark subjected to eighteen years of the grim tyranny her mother had described made her furious and afraid together. Hard common sense told her that she was unable to care for him herself, so she was forced to leave the small town in the Midlands and travel halfway across the world to Fiji.

It was when she was looking at Mark's birth certificate that she had conceived the notion of pretending that he was her son. It gave only his name, with no details of parentage. Common sense told her that she had little hope of getting away with the deceit for long, unless she could be so convincing that her grandfather didn't even bother to check. At least it was worth a try, for if Maurice Fowler accepted Mark for his great-grandson, he could have no claim upon him.

Secretly, when she turned twenty, she would apply for guardianship papers and once they were granted Mark would be safe.

It was a mad scheme, so full of holes that it could be wrecked if anyone bothered to make the simplest of checks. And of course, her grandfather might be so old-fashioned that he would throw her out into the proverbial snow, clutching her supposedly illegitimate child to her breast, but it offered Mark some hope of a decent life. So she had determined on it and would stick with it until proved a liar.

There was a lot going for it, too.

Mark's efforts to say 'Meredith' and his pronunciation of mother were not so far apart, and since their mother's death he had clung to his sister with all of the affection a child could be expected to show a parent. And they looked so alike—Mark a darker, masculine version of herself, with the same broad brow and wide eyes above high cheekbones which defined a firm mouth and very resolute, almost stubborn chin. Mark's jaw was wider, not like the pointed feature which lead to her nickname of 'cat-face' at school, but the resemblance was striking.

It was the chin which was her most prominent feature when the taxi disgorged them and their luggage outside her grandfather's house the next day. All the way up the long drive lined with magnificent raintrees she had found herself swallowing to keep down a hard dry lump which threatened to block her throat. Against her Mark slept, a hot little bundle tired by the ferry journey back to Lautoka, his fine hair in damp tendrils against the olive of his cheek. A fierce wave of protectiveness washed over her as she looked down at him. So defenceless a little being should not be left to the far from tender mercies of the man her mother had described to her as 'about as soft as granite and as understanding'.

But she could not prevent the hollow feeling in her stomach which preceded panic as the house came into sight, an enormous white place, Colonial style, single-storeyed with wide verandahs where orchids hung in lilac and rose and golden glory. Like Paradise, she thought, eyes widening as she gazed around the garden. Frangipani bloomed amidst lilies and more orchids in front of foliage lush enough to cool the riotous colours and provide a perfect background for the house. Life here must have been grim indeed for her mother to have left so much beauty with no regrets, so little yearning for the past.

## CHAPTER TWO

THE Fijian girl who opened the door obviously knew exactly who they were, for after that first startled glance she smiled radiantly and scooped the still sleeping Mark from Meredith's arms, murmuring, 'You've been a long time coming home, *marama*. Come in.'

The hall was huge, pale green silken wallpaper lit by an immense sunburst of a chandelier, but the room into which she was shown was a complete contrast, an office of such stark modernity that it almost made Meredith's eyes ache.

'Miss Colfax and the little boy, Mr Fowler,' her escort said.

Meredith's eyes flew to the man behind the desk. He

was big, with handsome reckless features schooled by self-control into ruthless authority, and the last time she had seen him was when he had passed them as Don kissed her the night before.

Her appearance must have been as much a shock to him as his was to her, but apart from the fact that his mouth hardened into a thin straight line, he showed no signs of it. Meredith knew that she had gone as white as a sheet; even as she collapsed into a chair beside the desk she wondered at the strength of her reaction.

'I'll take the baby,' the Fijian girl said, still cheerful and apparently unawed by the forbidding creature behind the desk.

But Meredith said sharply, 'No! He'll be upset if he wakes in a strange place.'

'Leave him, Litia, please. And you'd better warn Mr Fowler that they're here.'

Litia deposited Mark on a wide sofa, smiled down at him and then disappeared, swaying gracefully in her gold *sulu* and tunic.

Silence stretched between Meredith and the man behind the desk, a silence which made her heartbeats drum in her ears, a primitive rhythm of fear. At last, convinced that he was conducting a war of nerves, she looked up, her grey eyes enormous in the sensitive contours of her face.

'Just who are you?' she demanded, made arrogant by tension.

Black brows snapped together. 'A very distant connection of yours. Your great-grandfather and mine were cousins. You can work out the relationship if you like.'

'No, thank you,' she said crisply, trying for some command of the situation. 'Where is my grandfather?'

'After lunch he rests in his room. He's no longer as strong as he used to be.'

'He must hate that,' she observed. It was an odd conversation, with the memory of last night underlying the words.

'He's a realist, so he accepts it.' Beneath the dark brows his eyes were a strange tawny-gold, penetrating, keenly intelligent.

Meredith found herself thinking that eyes of such a colour should denote a warm, perhaps passionate nature; it was strange that they should be so cold.

Because the thought was vaguely disturbing, she hurried into speech, careless that she might sound rude. 'And just where do you fit in?'

His hard mouth curled. 'I run things,' he said smoothly. 'Your grandfather is old and his health is not good. He needs a general factotum.'

'You don't look like a factotum to me,' she said shrewdly. 'You look like the boss.'

The broad shoulders lifted in an arrogant shrug. 'Nobody is indestructible. Maurice has accepted that.'

Meredith said curtly, 'That doesn't sound like my grandfather.'

'What do you know of him? Only what your mother told you?'

The contempt in his voice brought her head up with a snap. How dared he speak of her mother like that! 'And you know nothing of *her*,' she commented bitterly.

'Only that she deliberately and wilfully broke her father's heart,' he returned with cold emphasis. 'And I suppose, like all those suffering from guilt, she eased it by bringing you up to think of him as a hard-hearted tyrant.'

Which was exactly how her mother had represented Maurice Fowler, but Meredith wasn't going to tell this arrogant cousin that!

With an aloof hauteur which she hadn't known she possessed she said, 'Until three months ago, Mr Fowler, I didn't know that my grandfather existed, so I wasn't brought up to think anything of him. As for being wilful and deliberate, to the best of my knowledge my mother never said or did anything to hurt anyone in her entire life. And you may take that for a fact.'

'I suppose running away from her father and her fiancé didn't constitute inflicting pain,' he observed sarcastically.

Meredith gave him a long, cool look. 'That,' she said without expression, 'depended entirely on what her father and fiancé felt for her, didn't it?' Not for worlds would she have let him see that the existence of a fiancé was news to her.

He nodded, those tawny eyes roving the fine lines and planes of her face as though trying to gauge her strengths and weaknesses. Against that impersonal searching glance Meredith had no defence but a studied blankness of expression which effectively drained the life and vitality from her features. After several moments of this superbly judged insolence she felt colour begin to rise through the layers of her skin. The pale grey of her eyes deepened, became irradiated with anger of a kind she had never before experienced, anger mixed with some unknown emotion which kept her pinned helplessly beneath that gaze like a rabbit before a snake. Unbidden the thought crept into her mind, this man is dangerous—in every way.

'After the clinch I saw you in last night it's a wonder you can still blush,' he remarked conversationally, almost smiling as he glanced down at something on his desk.

Meredith repressed her anger, realising instinctively that to lose her temper before this man would put her at an immense disadvantage.

'You have no right to comment on my actions,' she returned silkily, one slender hand tightening on the carved arm of her chair with the effort of keeping calm. 'My grandfather is my guardian, not you.'

As if he had not heard her he resumed coldly, 'I hope you didn't wake the child after you and your boy-friend got indoors. You both seemed in a hell of a hurry to get to a more secluded place.'

The innuendo made her feel sick, but on the point of indignantly refuting it she paused. And knew that he noted the hesitation before she said once more, 'You are not my guardian, Mr Fowler.'

If she were to claim Mark as her son it probably wouldn't do any harm to allow this man to think of her as promiscuous, however smirched she felt.

'Call me Dane,' he said, not bothering to hide his contempt. 'Perhaps now is the appropriate time to tell you that behaviour of that sort will not be condoned or permitted here. Fowler is a name well known throughout the South Pacific and although like all families we have had our black sheep, our women have so far managed to avoid any charge of loose morals.' He rose, surprising her again with his height, and walked around the desk to stand in front of her while his stare bored into her.

Meredith licked her lips, restraining herself with great difficulty from shrinking back into the chair. He loomed like some demonic Fate above her, and when his hands came down and fastened around her wrists to pull her up she flinched as if he had struck her.

He smiled grimly, those strange eyes holding hers as he spoke. 'So restrain your sexual urges while you're here, you little slut, or you'll be out on your ear so fast that you'll never see what hit you!'

Shaken to the core by the naked disgust in his voice, she found it impossible to breathe. Her pulse thudded heavily in her throat, lashes fluttering to hide the fear and awareness engendered by his proximity; she licked her lips again.

His eyes narrowed, became mere slits of frozen light in the deeply tanned face. 'And don't try any of your wiles on me,' he said softly, every word dropping into the terrible silence between them like sharp, hard stones. 'I'm rather fastidious as to my choice of lovers.'

For a moment those long fingers tightened cruelly on the fragile bones of her wrists, then, as if he could no longer bear to touch her, he almost pushed her back into the chair, turning away with a smooth economy of movement which revealed that the man was an athlete. Probably worked hard to keep that way too, Meredith thought when she could think again, whipping up fierce resentment to hide that moment of perilous awareness which had flashed between them. Yes, she would hate Dane Fowler, and he felt nothing but contempt for her, but for a moment he had seen her as a woman—and she had responded, forced to recognise that in spite of his hatefulness he possessed an aura of sexual magnetism which transcended almost everything else about him.

'So now you understand,' he said, turning around to face her across the desk. 'Your grandfather is prepared to accept you, but I'll make it my business to see that you toe the line. And in case you had any ideas about him, he's even less likely to be moved by any feminine tricks you might try to use. Like me he's had enough experience to recognise almost every one in the armoury.'

'I take it you're not married, Dane,' she replied sweetly.

For a moment his expression altered, as if she had startled him, but it hardened once more into a mask of cold composure. 'No. Nor am I engaged. For your further information, I do not hate women, nor do I find them irrelevant. And I have my normal share of instincts and needs.' His glance flicked up and down the length of her body, small and erect in the massive chair. 'I'm quite willing to admit that you are beautiful and no doubt very pleasant to make love to, but I have no intention of discovering just how pleasant. So don't waste your time and mine by trying to get around me that way.'

His glance snapped up to her face, probing, assessing. Muscles in her neck moved against the gleaming skin as she swallowed almost convulsively, but her lashes were lowered so that he could not read the expression in her eyes.

Perhaps it was the pallor of her cheeks which made him say somewhat less harshly, 'I'm sorry if I've been blunt, but it's best that you know exactly where you stand.'

'Of course,' Meredith returned tonelessly, resisting with every atom of will power her urge to snatch up the only ornament on the desk, a heavy Chinese porcelain deer, and hurl it at him to hit where it would do most damage. But resist she did; after all, she should be pleased that he had decided, without any prompting on her part, that she was promiscuous. It would make the lie she had decided to tell so much more credible. No doubt her grandfather would rely to some extent on Dane's judgment and if he thought it in character for her to have an illegitimate child then they might not probe very deeply into the past.

But did he suspect every couple he saw kissing of being lovers?

Litia, the maid, brought her to her feet once more by knocking.

'He's ready to see you both now,' she told Meredith. 'And you, Mr Fowler.' Once more she picked Mark up, her serene features softening. 'He's a good sleeper,' she murmured. 'And doesn't he look like you!'

'Yes, he does.' Glad that the resemblance had been remarked upon once more, and in Dane Fowler's presence, Meredith found herself being shown along yet another corridor, this one hung with paintings, some of which she would very much like to have considered more closely. But with Litia on one side and her remote fifteenth or something cousin on the other, she had no hope of slowing down.

I feel like someone being marched off to jail, she thought, trying to hide her growing anxiety with flippancy. Or escorted to an audience with Royalty. Or headed for the axe. All of them, probably, if her mother's father hadn't softened considerably over the past twenty years. From the way Dane Fowler had spoken of him he was still as hard as ever. But she would form her own impressions of the man first before deciding whether it would be necessary to unofficially adopt Mark as her son.

Maurice Fowler was still a big man, a man whose features expressed nothing so much as a tough ruthlessness. He had the pale grey eyes which were his legacy to his granddaughter, but whereas hers were clear and cool, his seemed to have iced over. Perhaps they softened when they rested on the sleeping child; Meredith was convinced that if they did it was merely a reflex, because most of humanity found it hard to resist a sleeping child, especially when the child was beautiful, like Mark.

However, after that swift revealing glance he fixed his eyes on Meredith, saying in a deep, harsh voice, 'You don't look much like a Fowler.'

It was obvious that he thought less of her for that. Meredith knew that if she allowed him to intimidate her she would lose any hope of freedom. Lifting her brows, she answered, 'My father's name was Colfax.'

There was an ominous silence before he barked, 'Sit down, all of you. Litia, give her the boy.'

Gratefully Meredith accepted the chair which Dane

indicated she should use, drawing comfort from Mark's warm little body against her as she looked around. The study was big, the walls darkly panelled wood, the floor covered in beautiful subdued Persian rugs. It was the furniture which spoiled it, great cumbersome bureaux and cupboards, and seating of such undistinguished Victorian mediocrity that it was almost chic. It looked as though no one had done anything to the place since the turn of the century. No wonder Maurice was hard, if this was his chosen milieu!

Fighting down a panic which could not be given rein, Meredith looked from one man to the other as Dane walked across to where Maurice Fowler sat. Yes, they both had that air of power, she thought, realising for the first time just what she had taken on. Defeating these two would be about the hardest thing she would ever have to do, but it would have to be accomplished if she was to make any sort of life for Mark.

'Your father's name is not to be spoken in this house,' her grandfather told her coldly when Litia had left the room.

'I am not in the habit of dragging it into every conversation,' she returned, 'but I have no intention of avoiding it.'

The hard old mouth tightened. 'If you don't like the way we do things here you can leave tomorrow.'

'I'll enjoy myself talking to gossip columnists,' she returned hardly, ignoring the way Dane Fowler watched her.

'Are you blackmailing me?'

She moved Mark gently. 'Yes. I didn't want to come here, but you insisted. I can't care for Mark as he should be cared for, so I was forced to obey. You don't want us, and we don't want to be here. But as we are, I'm not going to abandon the nineteen years I've already lived. And that includes my father's name.'

The cold eyes searched her face, trying to find any signs of weakness. Meredith met his gaze with composure, surprised to find that the fear which had been her constant companion since the day her mother had died had gone. She felt—almost liberated, she thought with amazement, as though she understood Maurice Fowler, and from now on the scattered fragments of her life would come together and make a pattern once more.

'Well, you've got loyalty,' he ackowledged grudgingly, adding with grim humour, 'but don't push your luck. It wouldn't be the first time I've figured as an ogre in newspaper columns and I daresay it won't be the last. Besides, I hold the ace in your pack. I said that you can go; I'll not let you take the boy. You just admitted that you can't care for him.'

'And how will you cope?' she asked, relieved that they had come to grips with the main problem so early in the piece. Darling Mark, to be called a problem!

The massive shoulders shrugged. 'As I did with your mother. The Fijians love children and make excellent nurses. But I'll not make the same mistakes I made with her. There'll be no weakness, no coddling; the boy will be brought up to take his place in the business and know what it means to be a Fowler.'

Meredith found that blood really could run cold. But she could not allow herself to be afraid now. With a level glance at him she returned, 'And where does that leave Dane?'

'Dane? Where he is, of course. He's my heir.' The old man smiled sardonically. 'Handpicked, Meredith, chosen because I can trust him completely. He has a brilliant brain and the kind of character needed to keep the business growing. Oh, Dane won't suffer.'

'And if Mark doesn't want to have anything to do with the business?'

'I allowed your mother her own way. I can't see that it did her any good. I suppose she did the same with you; that doesn't matter, but this boy will be brought up to understand what the word obedience means. He'll go away to school like Dane when he's eight or nine and learn to be a man.'

Meredith's gaze flicked up from her grandfather to rest on the face of the man behind him. Dane Fowler was leaning against the wall, his autocratic features schooled into a lack of expression which didn't fool her one bit. He was enjoying this. Through the cold anger that was beginning to possess her Meredith found herself betting her only silk stockings that he didn't know the meaning of the word obedience.

'And those are your plans for him?' she asked in a cool, remote little voice, as much of Dane as of her grandfather.

But it was the old man who spoke. 'Yes. He's my only male descendant. His parents amounted to nothing much, but there must be something of me in him, and by God I'll find it.'

'However much he suffers?'

Contemptuously he answered, 'Children are tough if they're allowed to be. Don't try to fill my ears with your modern psychological rubbish; I don't believe a word of it.'

'And yet I'll bet you're a pretty good psychologist yourself,' she observed calmly. 'I should imagine that a business man would need to be. It's just that because it's instinctive you don't recognise it. However, that's nothing to do with the point.'

'Which is?'

It was Dane who spoke, his bored tones belied by the flashing glance which he directed at her.

Meredith took a deep breath, looking down at the soft unconsciousness of Mark's sleeping face.

'The point is that Mark is not yours to dispose of,' she said as matter-of-factly as she could. 'He's mine—my son.'

There was a moment of silence during which she lifted her head and looked directly at her grandfather. The proud features remained without expression, but there was something about the rigid old figure which told her that she had dealt him an immense blow. She dared not look at Dane.

A long moment later, as if suddenly released from a spell her grandfather twisted in his chair, demanding harshly, 'Do you believe her?'

'Yes.'

It came out without any hesitation. Well, kisses had brought down kingdoms before; it was a minor matter which that one kiss with Don had accomplished this time. Merely tarnished her reputation irreparably.

'I see.'

Apparently that ended matters, for Maurice turned back to her, his expression heavy with disgust, the iced grey eyes sliding contemptuously over her and the child in her arms. Almost she tightened her grip on Mark as if to protect him.

'Do you happen to know who the father is?' he asked with corrosive sarcasm.

'Yes.'

'Who, then?'

She remained silent, her mind casting around for the least distasteful alternative. After a moment she said quietly, 'He was a boy at school. It doesn't matter about him. He's at university now.'

Very, very slightly the strain in her grandfather's expression eased. 'Clever?'

Well, her father had been brilliant, so her mother had said. He had just never been able to settle.

'Yes,' she admitted.

'Does he know?'

Which would be the best answer here? And must he put her through this inquisition with Dane in the same room? Blushing as if her story were true, she said half under her breath, 'No.'

'I see.' He got up then, stiffly but without help from Dane, and with heavy tread came across to where she sat clutching the child. 'Let me see him,' he ordered harshly.

Mark's head was pressed against her shoulder. Very gently she turned his face; the movement pulled back the neat collar of her dress to expose the rounded swell of her breast. Colour rose across her cheekbones, but she managed to twitch the fabric back into place without disturbing Mark. Looking up, she met the full force of Dane Fowler's gaze, coldly ironic, and this time blushed in real earnest.

'The father was dark?'

Meredith met her grandfather's eyes squarely. 'Yes,' she said, justifying her lie by implication with the thought that her father had had black hair.

'I can see the resemblance,' said Maurice Fowler, and then fiercely, 'Have you told anyone here?'

'No.'

'Or at Hibiscus Island?' Dane's voice was almost bored.

Her grandfather swung around. 'What's this?'

'Tell him, Meredith.'

Damn him, she thought furiously, damn him, damn him, *damn him!* Not that she had intended to keep her stay there a secret, but she had an instinctive feeling that Maurice Fowler had had enough. So with a stony glance at the man just behind her grandfather she told him.

'We've been staying there for the past ten days. And I didn't tell anyone that Mark is my son, although I'm sure that they all thought he was.'

'That makes no difference,' Maurice said harshly. 'You're sure? No confidences, no feminine gossip sessions?'

'No.'

He moved away then, back to his own chair. 'Then we can let the original story stand. Oh,' as she opened her mouth, 'you shut up, miss. I've no intention of bandying any further words with you. While you're here the boy is your brother, and that's an end to it.'

Then he did something which revealed that he was an old, tired man. When his head touched the back of the chair he closed his eyes momentarily. Just that, yet as if it was a sign Dane moved, scooped Mark from Meredith's arms and with an imperious jerk of his head ordered her to follow him as he strode across towards the door.

Astonished, Meredith rose, but found that she could not just leave her grandfather, a lonely embittered man, rigid in his rigid chair, in his dark room.

Swiftly, before her nerve deserted her, she said quietly, 'Thank you,' and then fled, sure that if he looked towards her he would see her guilt emblazoned on her features.

# CHAPTER THREE

Mark awoke, hot, sticky and grumpy as was usual after an afternoon sleep, his feet hitting the floor with a thud.

'Meddy?' he called anxiously. 'Meddy?' which was his attempt at her name.

'I'm here, darling,' Meredith appeared in the doorway between their two rooms. 'Do you want a drink?'

'Yes.'

Pouring a glass of the fruit juice which Litia had left in a covered jug on the bureau, Meredith gave it to him, watching somewhat anxiously as he drank it thirstily down. Within a few moments he recovered his normally sweet temperament, smiling widely at her as he gave back the glass before asking, 'Where we are, Meddy?'

'This is Grandfather's house, and this is your bedroom. Would you like to have a look at mine? It's just through this door.'

'O.K.,' he said cheerfully, taking the hand she extended to him.

They had been given adjoining rooms in a wing of the house which extended away from the main block. A short passage linked them, with a bathroom on one side of it and a large dressing room on the other. Both bedrooms opened out on to a wide tiled verandah supported by graceful painted pillars. Obviously an addition, the wing had been built of concrete instead of the wood which was the fabric of the main house, yet oddly enough the two seemed to blend pleasantly.

Outside on the verandah it was cool, the air filtering through a mass of flowers and wide-leaved foliage plants which bordered it. There were orchids and several tall tree-ferns, a creeper which flung its large white, golden-throated flowers with insouciance along the edge of the verandah roof. When they followed a path between ferns and ginger plants, Meredith realised why this wing had been given to them for walls, high and almost hidden by further plantings and creepers, turned their back yard into a courtyard. Very safe for small children, thought Meredith wryly, noting that there was a door in the wall. The handle was too high for Mark to reach yet; reconnaissance revealed that it was locked. In one corner of the court the feathery velvet of a poinciana tree cast a shade which would be relished by whoever sat in the chairs beneath it; in another there was a small replica of a village *bure* except that it had no walls. Beneath the thatched roof Meredith had set out those toys of Mark's which she had brought from home.

'Look!' he squealed when he saw them. 'Mine things!'

Pretending surprise, she joined him, glad to have something to take her mind from the depressing memories of both of the interviews she had endured. Because Dane Fowler's condemnation had left a sore place in her emotions she forced herself to face it, acknowledging that by claiming Mark for her son she had exposed herself to his justifiable contempt.

Except that the contempt had been there first, well before her lie about Mark. Reluctantly she supposed that the kiss he had seen had probably looked less innocent than it was, especially when Don had seized her hand and run her up to the *bure*, but even so, he had no proof that she was promiscuous. He had just jumped to that conclusion. Which was rather odd for a man whose business must involve exactly the opposite quality. Perhaps, she thought frivolously as she left Mark to hammer pegs through a board and made her way to the chairs beneath the tree, perhaps he just considered women the inferior sex and there was nothing personal in his contempt at all. What a delightful prospect! Life with her grandfather would not have been easy at any time, but Dane Fowler was an added complication she could well do without.

She and Mark would just have to adopt a low profile, she told herself, unaware that the glowing spirit which irradiated her features and made them beautiful prevented any such thing.

Towards sunset she took Mark inside, bathed him in the tiled bathroom and put him into pyjamas. A small meal had been left on a tray in his room; when he had eaten she read him a story and sang 'Baa Baa, Black Sheep' before popping him into bed. Within a few seconds of bidding her goodnight he was asleep, arms outstretched in the innocent abandon of childhood.

Meredith bent, kissed his cheek and pulled the mosquito net down, her heart expanding with the force of her love for him. Any sacrifice, she thought passionately, was worth it if it would give him the happy childhood he deserved.

Buoyed up by this thought, she went into her own room. Litia had told her that she would call for her at seven o'clock and take her along to where her grandfather and Dane met before dinner. Before then she had to shower and discover where her clothes had been put. Being waited on was an odd business, she decided as she pulled out drawers in the dressing room; she was not sure that she liked it.

But the shower cooled and refreshed her, and when she had slipped on a deep pink dress which gave a little colour to the pale silky gold of her skin and climbed into high sandals the exact colour of the dress, she decided that no one could object to her appearance. Her arms and shoulders were covered so not even the censorious Dane would find anything to lift those straight brows at!

The room Litia led her to was elegant, with a pale Chinese rug covering the floor, furniture which bore the sophisticated imprint of the East and a fabulous silk hanging on one wall portraying an idealised Chinese landscape.

Her grandfather was sitting in a Chinese Chippendale chair; he glanced up as she came into the room but said nothing. Across the room by the window Dane Fowler stood looking out at the dark garden. He swung around when she appeared at the doorway, those amber eyes curiously penetrating. Neither man smiled, but after a moment Maurice asked, 'Is he asleep?'

'Yes,' she answered with composure.

'One of the girls, Renadi, is going to keep an eye on him in case he wakes. Do you drink?'

'If you're offering me one, I'll have a small dry sherry.' Without looking at him she sat down in the chair Dane indicated, waited with outward calmness while her grandfather glowered and his heir poured. The start of a lovely evening, she thought ironically.

Actually it wasn't so bad. Whatever their attitude to the rest of humanity, both men could produce the kind of superlative manners which smoothed social contacts. They discussed politics and sport, books, and to Meredith's astonishment, art; later she realised that the paintings in the hall should have warned her that her grandfather was a collector. The local politics meant nothing to her, but she held up her end when it came to books and art, and had the subtle pleasure of surprising them by the pertinacity of her occasional remarks.

The meal was served in an enormous dining room; superlative food, superlatively served, and after that it was time to return to the Chinese room. Promptly at ten, her grandfather had a small whisky and after it had gone he said goodnight and went out through the door, a tall, indomitable old figure, hard as nails but at least, she thought, interesting.

And that left her alone in the same room with Dane Fowler, who was looking bored and aloof and very handsome, if you liked tanned men with features carved from stone.

For herself, Meredith didn't, but she was sensible enough to realise that life was going to be extremely uncomfortable if they didn't reach some sort of working arrangement. After all, they were both going to live in the same house for an unknown time; even if they did dislike each other heartily it shouldn't be too hard to compromise.

Oddly enough he seemed to have reached the same conclusion, for he said abruptly, 'I noticed that you very carefully avoided addressing me directly tonight. For Maurice's sake I think we had better accept each other's presence with some degree of cheerfulness. I don't need to tell you that he's a sick man.'

'No, you don't,' she said. 'Is it his heart?'

He shrugged. 'I don't know. He's not the sort to confide, but he's been active all his life and he finds the restrictions he's forced to obey very frustrating. I can see no
reason to add to his burden.'

'If you could see a reason, would you?' she asked, waiting to see if he was really as pompous as he sounded.

He smiled, although his gaze was very hard. 'I'll leave
that for you to discover, if you're interested.'

'Oh, I'm interested, all right.' She had meant to sound
sarcastic, but perhaps she had failed, for she saw derision
leap into his expression.

'Don't push your luck, sweet cousin. And don't mis-
judge me; I may not be married or engaged, but I'm not
available.'

Red temper hazed her sight; fighting to keep control of
it took all her energy so that her voice was colourless as
she replied, 'Don't worry, Dane, you're not my type.'

'No, you like them young,' he agreed smoothly. 'I hope
that by now you've learnt to take precautions. Your
grandfather would have no hesitation in getting rid of
you if you're pregnant once more. One illegitimate great-
grandchild he might accept, but I doubt if he'd be as
complaisant if you presented him with another.'

'Don't worry,' she gritted, hands clasped so tightly in
her lap that the knuckles shone white. 'I promise you I'm
not pregnant.'

'Good.' Not that he sounded as if he believed her. 'I
didn't expect you to be, I'll admit.'

'Why?'

He smiled again, letting his eyes wander over her tight
expression with insolent freedom. 'Well, let's say that to
take a risk like that again you'd have to be a fool, and
you're not a fool, are you, Meredith?'

Just what did he mean by that? For a moment she
thought she read some kind of secret amusement in the
depths of his eyes, as though he knew of her lie, but although she scanned his face with strained intensity she
could not be sure. After a moment she answered sulkily,
'I hope not.'

'Good.'

Almost as if they had reached some agreement. Meredith swallowed, trying to hide her suspicion that the conversation had run away from her. Dane was looking down into the depths of his whisky glass, and yes, he was smiling a little, the corners of his mouth tilted into what, she became convinced, would turn out to be an extremely unpleasant expression. When at last he drained the glass and set it down he turned to look at her, but those strong features were expressionless, only the leaping lights in his eyes betraying the keen intelligence which animated the brain behind that splendid mask.

'You look puzzled,' he remarked. 'Have I said something?'

Two could play at that game. 'Only implied that I'm not stupid,' she returned, very smoothly.

'Why should that surprise you?'

'Oh, just that I thought, after this afternoon, that I had no admirable attributes at all.' Maliciously eager to break through his monumental self-confidence, she gave no thought to the implications of what she had said.

He lifted his brows at this, very assured, more than a little bored. 'My dear girl, if you're fishing for compliments then I'll tell you that you're obviously intelligent, obviously beautiful, obviously spirited. Seen in a wet *sulu* you have the sort of body which makes any man take note. I'd be lying if I didn't admit that I could quite easily desire you. If you remember, I said as much this afternoon. However, I'm not a fool, and nor am I so enslaved by my physical needs that I'd forget everything I've ever known about women and embark on an affair with you. The sooner you realise that the better it will be for all of us. Have I made myself clear?'

Beneath the stinging scorn in his voice and expression Meredith felt herself growing pale. How he must despise her, to speak so scathingly!

Clutching at her pride, she rose to her feet, saying thinly, 'More than clear. Either you have the conceit of the devil or you're so afraid of my attractions that you need a bludgeon to frighten me off. As we're being so frank I'll just make one thing clear too. Believe me, I'm not lusting after you, Dane. When I want a man I'll find someone who's more than a flesh-and-blood computer with a nice line in insults.' Almost blinded by angry tears, she made her way to the door, but stopped to fling over her shoulder, 'I wouldn't sleep with you if you were the last man on earth! So now you can relax. *Goodnight!*'

With a dignity which she hadn't known she possessed she walked through the door and down the hall, half dreading to hear him come up behind her. However, she made it to her own room without meeting anyone else and collapsed into an armchair, aware that her legs were trembling with reaction.

An ugly scene indeed! But she couldn't regret her words. How dared he treat her like that? She hated him, and always would hate him. It was a pity that for her grandfather's sake she would have to pretend to get on reasonably well with him. With any luck she needn't see very much of him. Presumably he spent most of the day at work in that office of his; perhaps he even had another in Lautoka.

When he didn't appear at the breakfast table the next morning she discovered that he had eaten early and been driven to the airport, from whence he would fly across to Suva, the administrative capital on the other side of the island.

'He'll be back tonight for dinner,' Maurice told her. 'As a matter of fact we're having guests. Have you a dress you can wear?'

'Of course I have.'

He looked at her from beneath his brows. 'I mean something good, something that will give you confidence. The girl Dane is thinking of marrying will be here; she's a beauty, and she dresses well.'

Meredith decided that perhaps he had not intended his words to sound so insulting. 'I have two dinner dresses, one short and one long. Both are of quite good quality, but neither will put me in the princess class,' she told him, helping Mark with an obstreperous piece of golden paw-paw.

He frowned as if her reply displeased him. 'Choose the

one you feel best in, then. When we go to Australia next you'd better buy some good clothes,' he said abruptly.

Meredith's eyes were large, but astonishment widened them even further. 'Thank you,' she said stiffly, adding with an effort, 'You're very kind.'

'I'm not, and you know it. You're a Fowler here, and you'll dress like one. And behave like one,' he said grimly. 'That involves decent clothes. I'll make you an allowance which should cover anything you might need. Dane is seeing to it. If you can't cope see him about it.'

Firmly vowing to keep within that allowance even if it meant wearing rags, Meredith thanked him once more, which seemed to make him even more withdrawn.

After breakfast she and Mark explored the place, discovering that the garden was so exquisitely planned and cared for that it seemed, like some English parks, the quintessence of naturalness. But far removed from those English parks was the riotous exuberance of the growth, the tropical enthusiasm of everything from the immense spreading banyan which dominated a paved area of the garden to the crotons, bushes with leaves more vivid than many a flower, green, gold, pink, scarlet and bronze dotted and splotched with contrasting hues in a fantasy of colour. And the flowers! Hibiscuses all shades of red and yellow, the trailing bougainvillea in lilacs and pinks and mauves, frangipani of all colours, orchids and zinnias and margiolds, all backed by trees and shrubs which she had never seen before.

Spectacular was really the only word one could use for it; it looked like every romantic image of a tropical garden come to life.

'Pretty,' said Mark, stroking the wide golden blossom of an allamanda vine.

'Beautiful,' she agreed, looking through an archway covered with tiny heart-shaped panicles of pink flowers which revealed a swimming pool set amidst tiles as green as the grass they displaced.

'Swim?' Mark suggested as they made their way towards the pool, admiring the wrought iron chairs and tables, the elegant little cabana shaded by the plumed branches of a breadfruit tree.

Meredith agreed that a swim would be a lovely idea, and together they ran through the gathering heat to get their clothes.

It was a lazy, peaceful day. They swam, ate fruit that Litia brought out to them and drank mightily, fruit juice for Mark, iced tea for Meredith. It could have been any day at an empty resort, for apart from lunch they saw nothing of Maurice. But there was Litia, and Renadi, the girl who had kept her eye on Mark, and a man called Joseph who swept the lawn with a brush made of coconut fibres, and another one called Matiu who was pruning a tree in one of the borders, all of them keenly interested in Mark and more than a little interested in Meredith.

At last Mark was asleep in his bed and Meredith regarded herself in the floor-length mirror in her bedroom, a frown marring the smoothness of her forehead. Honesty forced her to admit that she looked somewhat drab in the honey-coloured jersey dress which had seemed so smart in England. In the tropics one could indulge a taste for vivid colours without appearing at all garish.

Never mind, she comforted herself. The dress clung softly to her body, lovingly emphasising the long clean lines, the barely adult curves. Were she much heavier those curves would be too much; a pound or so less on her frame would make it into a mere covering without style or shape. She wore the deep pink sandals, their high heels giving her confidence, and a pair of rose quartz earrings which had been a gift from her father to her mother. Very carefully she touched her eyelids with shadow, coloured her lips and sprayed on the only extravagance she had purchased in one of Nandi's duty-free shops, 'Miss Dior' perfume, its woodsy fragrance cooling on the hot heavy air.

'You'd better go now,' Renadi told her from the connecting door.

For some reason butterflies took wing in Meredith's stomach. 'How do I look?' she asked, pirouetting.

'Nice,' the Fijian girl said somewhat shyly. She meant it, however, which was a comfort.

After taking a last peep at Mark Meredith set off towards the drawing room, only to find Dane coming to meet her, his expression set in the lines of boredom she so disliked.

Tension prickled along her nerves. 'Am I late?' she asked quickly.

'No, but your grandfather is getting impatient.'

Which probably meant that he wanted to make sure that her clothes wouldn't disgrace them. Pride lifted Meredith's chin, gave a flashing vitality to her expression as she walked into the room, her sandals bringing her chin up to the level of Dane's shoulder. The sound of her heels tapping across the parquet floor gave her confidence a lift too; they were Italian, her sandals, her last extravagance chosen a year ago to wear to a ball.

Awareness of her grandfather's scrutiny helped her sustain her progress the length of the room. Just like being presented to Royalty, she thought, an impish smile curling the corners of her mouth. Almost she had to prevent herself from curtseying as they came up to where he was seated in a square black chair, his erect posture setting his years at bay.

He made no attempt to hide his scrutiny, but after a moment said, 'You'll do. You've more style than—than many.' Turning his head, he said something in Fijian to the man who waited behind him. Beside her Meredith sensed rather than felt Dane stiffen, but a fleeting glance at him revealed nothing more than the stark lines of his profile.

'Sit down,' Maurice Fowler ordered. 'How is the child?'

'In an earthquake he just might wake,' Meredith told him, sinking on to the edge of the modern sofa. 'He sleeps like a log.'

'Joseph tells me that he can swim.'

Somewhat startled by the fact that this autocratic man thought nothing of gossiping with one of his gardeners, Meredith agreed, adding with a hint of mischief, 'He can also climb trees, and his constant chattering drives people to wear ear-plugs.'

'I've ordered a tricycle for him,' he told her curtly, accepting sherry from Dane.

Meredith frowned. 'I don't want to sound ungrateful, but I'd rather you didn't shower him with toys. He's quite happy with the ones he's got.'

'Afraid I'll spoil him?' He smiled grimly. 'I'll buy him what I want, miss, and there's nothing you can do about it.'

For some reason he was goading her into an argument. Meredith folded her lips tight, refusing to give him the pleasure of provoking her. Fortunately Dane came across with a drink for her, something long and cold and definitely non-alcoholic, and a few moments afterwards the Fijian he had sent on an errand came back into the room carrying a small box which he gave to Maurice.

'This was your mother's,' he said, opening it and hauling out a ring box as if the thing scalded his fingers. 'It will go with your earrings.'

The stone glittered in its setting of diamonds, an unusual pale pink but with the fire and brilliance of its companion jewels. Meredith stared at it, her breath held in her throat.

'What is it?' she asked.

'A rose diamond.'

For a moment she was fascinated by the beautiful, fantastic thing, but loyalty to her mother made her close the box with a decisive snap. She looked across at her grandfather, but found her eyes caught by the Fijian man behind his chair. He was nodding, urging her to accept with a frown of anxiety between his brows. From beneath her lashes Meredith cast a look of unconscious appeal at Dane, saw the slight inclination of his head.

Slowly she opened the box again, took out the lovely glittering thing and slid it on to the finger of her right hand, murmuring, 'Thank you.'

'One of these days I'll tell you how I got it,' her grandfather remarked ironically. 'It's too long a story to go into here. I think I can hear people arriving.'

A dozen sat down to dinner, most of them middle-aged or elderly apart from Meredith, Dane and the woman whom Maurice had said he would marry, one Ginny Moore who arrived with her mother, a slender, exquisitely dressed women who, it became obvious, was also very much in favour of an engagement. Mother and daughter had identical eyes, blue the colour of the sea, which delivered equally identical measuring glances at Meredith as they were introduced.

Apart from that they had little in common, Mrs Moore being a vague lady with an interest in the arts, while her daughter was very modern, very up-to-date, with an opinion about everything.

Astounded at her uncharitable feelings, Meredith took herself well in hand; it was not difficult to be pleasant, for while Maurice's contemporaries were clearly curious they accepted her with an equanimity which said a lot for maturity. But Ginny Moore.... Somehow Meredith could not rid herself of the idea that Miss Moore had disliked her at sight. What made things worse was the fact that she had a horrid suspicion that she reciprocated wholeheartedly.

Not that such a reaction should be surprising. After all, anyone who was as devoted to Dane as Ginny showed herself to be must be attuned to him, which meant that she would automatically dislike those he disliked. And nothing could be clearer than his dislike of Meredith Colfax!

To her considerable dismay Meredith found that she occupied the hostess's place at the table. She could only hope that she acquitted herself satisfactorily. Fortunately everyone knew everyone else, so she was not forced to help out with conversation; indeed, they all indulged in extremely animated discussions with no hiatus to set her brains cudgelling for another subject to get them going again. A glance round the table revealed that she and her grandfather were by far the least talkative. He sat, eating little as he listened with a slight smile to the chatter around him, his eyes roving from one to the other in shrewd assessment.

Dane surprised Meredith. Possessed as he was of just as much charisma as Maurice, the evening revealed him to be worldly and experienced, a worthy heir apparent but not of the same mould, for he was very much his own man; it became clear to Meredith that although Maurice might have picked him to follow in his footsteps he could have got there by his own endeavour. He had the same indefinable air of authority that sat on Maurice's shoulders, but combined with it was an effortless sophistication which enhanced the basic strength of the man. And nothing, not even that sexual charisma, could hide the brilliance of the mind behind those handsome features, she decided wisely, watching as he charmed an elderly woman into complete submission.

The conversation swirled around her, while on her finger the rose diamond winked and twinkled, a constant reminder of her place in this household. Unconsciously she saw the room as a painting and in her mind began to sketch in the various figures, noting attitudes and colours, the crimson of the hibiscus flowers in a snake of greenery down the centre of the table, the same colour picked up in the candles and table napkins, the silver candelabra reflecting the cutlery.

'You're very quiet, Meredith,' Ginny Moore said, her voice startlingly loud in the first pause in the conversation. 'Are you tired?'

Immediately Meredith felt haggish and boorish.

'Not at all,' she replied politely, meeting the opaque blue of the woman's eyes with fortitude.

'Perhaps we're boring you, then?' She smiled, the beautifully made up mask of her face unaffected by warmth or interest. 'I'm sure that when I was a teenager I would have found a gathering such as this very dull.'

Meredith had the usual dislike of being patronised, but some intuition deep within her warned her that Miss Moore was being more than patronising, she was being directly antagonistic.

'Really?' Meredith allowed herself to look faintly astonished, aware that both Dane and her grandfather were watching them. With a deprecating smile she continued, 'No, I'm not at all bored. Awed is probably a better word. I like good conversation, but unless I've something to contribute I prefer to listen rather than disturb the flow with inane remarks.'

Those eyes widened, then narrowed, and for a moment

Ginny looked far from beautiful as the implication of Meredith's remarks hit home. But she had immense self-control, for even as the patches of red beneath her make-up faded she returned sweetly:

'How sensible of you.' Turning to Dane, she said with a hint of laughter in her voice, 'My dear, your little cousin is truly a Fowler, don't you think? Quite unafraid of speaking out and with very definite opinions.'

Already beginning to regret her impulsive remark, Meredith could have kicked herself when he replied unemotionally, 'Time will tell, Ginny,' with a smile which could only be construed as dismissive.

It was an effort for Meredith to repress her desire to look at her grandfather, but she managed to do it. She would not glance his way as if anxious about his reactions. Independence, she told herself, was a thing of the mind, and the fact that she was dependent on him for a home need not make her rely on him in any other way. Unless she wished, no one could force her to give up her emotional and mental independence. And she most emphatically did not wish.

It was interesting to see how Ginny Moore treated Dane. Too clever to agree with him about everything, she yet made it clear that while they might disagree on details, when it came to fundamentals they were basically in accord—thereby, Meredith thought cynically, showing him that their minds and characters were in tune; any differences were minor, ensuring that a life together would not be dull.

Very clever, but if that was what had to be done to acquire a husband Meredith rather thought she would prefer to remain single, for she was convinced that the real Ginny Moore was well hidden from sight behind that exquisite mask. Surely after a while the repression must become too much, with shattering results!

After dinner there was coffee, served with liqueurs out on the verandah beneath a canopy of sensuously perfumed orchids.

'Sit by me,' Maurice commanded half beneath his breath as they made their way out.

Meredith allowed herself to be put into a cane chair, relaxing into the plump cushions with a sigh of delight, for the night sky enchanted her. Here in the South Pacific the stars seemed close enough to steal, huge jewels embedded in a sky of blue-black velvet, while the moon rose over the enormous volcanic cliffs behind them like a rough disc of silver, the markings on its face clearer than ever they had been at home.

'The atmosphere's clearer,' her grandfather said when she commented on it. 'Have you seen the Southern Cross?'

'I found it the first night I was here. Why is it called a cross? It has five stars, and really it looks more like a kite, I think.'

He actually laughed at that. 'Hush, girl, that's blasphemy! For that matter, what other constellations look like their names? Are you interested in the stars?'

'You could hardly help it, living here,' she said. 'I mean, they're so close they're almost oppressive, aren't they?'

'They can get that way,' he said somewhat grimly. 'Did you enjoy working in that bank?'

Considerably startled by the abrupt change of subject, she stammered slightly in her answer. 'Y-yes, I did. At least——'

'Well?' he prompted after a moment as she still hesitated.

'Well, it was better than teaching would have been,' she said defiantly.

He smiled again but said nothing further, turning instead to a couple who had been conversing in low tones beside them. Apparently he had discovered whatever it was that he wanted to know, for from then on until the end of the evening he ignored her, although several times, as she moved among the guests, Meredith felt his gaze on her.

The party broke up comparatively early, and within a very few minutes Maurice made his way towards his bedroom, leaning somewhat heavily on the arm of the Fijian who found the ring earlier in the evening. Maurice introduced him as Vasilau, and said as they shook hands, 'You'll see a lot of him, Meredith. He looks after me.'

Like all Fijians Vasilau had a smile as big as his hands, but the dark eyes were as shrewd in their kindly way as Maurice's. In the short time she had been in Fiji Meredith had discovered that although the people lived up to their reputation for complete and charming good humour, they were not the simple children of nature her mother had led her to expect. Possessed of immense personal dignity and considerable intelligence, they saw nothing menial in service; indeed, she rather thought that the idiosyncrasies of those they served provided them with much appreciated amusement. Certainly they seemed to derive a keen enjoyment from their jobs. The girls on Hibiscus Island had treated the guests as friends, which was the same attitude her grandfather's staff assumed towards her. And in the look she saw on Vasilau's face as he helped her grandfather to his feet there was something of the affection of a son.

For some reason this made her feel happier. Not, she told herself, that she had any reason to feel sorry for the old autocrat, who had what he wanted, power and wealth, but it was good to know that he inspired regard as well as respect.

Pensively she made her way to her room, checking that Mark was still asleep on the way. Dane had taken the Moore females home so she did not have to worry about meeting him. Cowardly though it might be, she felt that it was a good idea to retire before he arrived home so that there could be no possible chance of a tête-à-tête. It would be just his style to take her to task for her largely unintentional rudeness to his nasty bride-to-be. Thinking happily that he and his Ginny suited each other extremely well, she stripped off her make-up and went to bed.

Unfortunately, when she and Mark arrived at the breakfast table, there was no one else but Dane there, and judging by the thin-lipped smile he proffered her, he would far rather have been alone. For some reason Meredith had woken in a lighthearted mood, and the cool reception to her greeting made her hide a grin.

'Gorgeous weather,' she observed cheerfully, as she popped Mark into his high chair.

'About average for this time of year.'

Goodness, he *was* grumpy! Meredith helped Mark to cereal, then spooned passionfruit juice over the rich apricot flesh of a paw-paw, wondering covertly just how old Dane was. He acted about ninety, but he looked to be only around thirty, if that.

A very handsome thirty, she had to admit, even if a trifle harsh-featured. Not her style at all. Looks and magnetism were all very well, but combined with intelligence and the kind of hard intolerance which seemed to be his outstanding characteristic, they became overpowering. He was a hypocrite, too, despising her for promiscuous behaviour, yet revealing last night that he had had loads of experience with women. And not all of it platonic, she knew as clearly as if he had told her. The old double standard! Or perhaps what he despised was what he saw as her lack of discretion. So he was a double hypocrite!

Deciding that she disliked men who made her skin prickle, Meredith ate her breakfast in demure silence, speaking only to Mark, who, not at all intimidated by the dour silence from the other side of the table, talked and chuckled and behaved perfectly normally.

Just as she was pouring out coffee for them both Vasilau materialised in the doorway.

'Miss Meredith, can you come with me, please?' he asked.

'Yes, yes, of course.'

But she hesitated for a moment until Dane said drily, 'I won't eat him, you know. He'll be all right.'

Feeling stupid, she nodded, said, 'Be good for a little while,' to Mark and then followed Vasilau into the hallway.

'Your grandfather wants to see you,' he told her, smiling broadly enough to drive away the tiny crease between her brows.

'Is he all right?'

'Yes, he's good.' He sounded surprised as if Maurice Fowler was made out of cast-iron. 'Just has something to say.'

What he had to say was short and to the point. 'You can take over the running of the house,' he told her, glowering at her from beneath his heavy brows. 'Taufa wants to go home to be with her grandchildren and it will give you something to do. She'll come along to the morning room after breakfast and you can talk to her then.'

On the whole Meredith, although taken aback, was not unwilling. She knew nothing whatsoever about keeping house, but she had youth's optimism and hoped that she would soon learn. So her response was cheerful.

Possibly a little too cheerful, for her grandfather said grimly, 'You'll have to keep an eye on things, you know; plan meals and that sort of thing.'

'There'll be a few mistakes, but not ever the same one twice,' she assured him.

To her surprise he smiled. 'In that case you'll do. Now get back to your breakfast.'

Apparently it was to be a day of surprises, for in the morning room Dane was wiping Mark's cheeks with a skill which denoted an old hand at the game. And Mark, instead of wriggling and complaining as he usually did, sat quite still, his dark eyes fixed with worshipful intensity on the autocratic features above him.

Neither looked up as Meredith came into the room, but when Dane had put the table napkin down Mark smiled cherubically and said, 'Thank you, man.'

And Dane smiled back, the stern lines of his face softening into humour. 'You'll do,' he said, touching the small chin with a lean forefinger.

Well! Meredith knew that her astonishment was written across her features; to hide it she drank deeply of orange juice and inevitably choked on a drop of it. By the time she had mopped up both males were looking at her with exactly the same quizzical expression so that she laughed, her eyes alight with amusement.

Mark responded immediately, clapping his hands together as he chuckled; for a moment Meredith thought that Dane might join him, but apparently she was not to be forgiven. As his features hardened she felt chilled by the obvious rebuff, and the laughter died from her eyes.

'Thank you for looking after Mark,' she said formally.

'Five minutes' supervision hardly constitutes reason for thanks,' he returned, dismissal obvious in his voice. 'By the way, Ginny is coming up this afternoon.'

'Oh.' Meredith could think of nothing to say, but after a long few seconds she added with a lameness which must be only too obvious, 'That's kind of her.'

'Yes, it is. Like me, she has little time for pert adolescents, but she feels that life could be dull for you here if you aren't introduced to a few young people. I believe she'll have someone with her.'

Meredith sent him a swift, sparkling look. 'How *very* kind of her,' she said softly, hiding her chagrin beneath her bland manner.

He was not fooled. Without altering his tone of voice at all he said, 'I'm glad you think so. Make sure that you restrain any impulse to score her off. Her manners are excellent, so you needn't fear any retaliation, but I have no such inhibitions.'

'How protective!' she marvelled, refusing to offer any excuse for last night's incident. 'Don't worry, I don't initiate, I only retaliate. If she's nice to me I'll be nice to her.'

The hard glance flicked across her face, but somewhat to her surprise he contented himself with saying grimly, 'I needn't, I hope, say that you'll be very much an object of interest, or that everyone will be watching to see what sort of person you are. The way you behave will be a direct reflection on your mother.'

Meredith watched as he rose, her expression withdrawn, hiding any emotion, her glance very cool and clear. He smiled at Mark, nodded across the table and left, very much master of the situation. An excellent psychologist, she had to own. That last remark had found her weakest spot, almost guaranteeing good behaviour in the future. Not for the world and all that was in it would she give anyone cause to carp at her mother's memory.

Dane Fowler was a clever man; ruthless, too. It would pay not to forget that.

With a sudden access of protective love she kissed Mark, hugged his warm little body until he protested, then, hand in hand, went with him to the dining room where Tafau waited.

The interview was short, with the housekeeper assuring Meredith that she would stay for a month to settle her in, before conducting her on a tour over the house with all the pride of one who has worked hard to achieve a desired result.

It was lovely, one of the few old Colonial houses left, but so well modernised that it was extremely comfortable, furnished by someone who had an excellent eye for style and line. Much of the furniture came from the East; Meredith was awed by exquisite silk screens and superb Chinese porcelain, touched with loving fingers a Korean medicine chest and the smooth patina of a magnificent Chinese bed in one of the guest bedrooms. Whoever had collected this harvest of beauty together had provided settings which enhanced the furniture but came very near to making a museum of the house. It was saved from excessive formality by flowers, dignified orchids, gay, brash hibiscus and the smooth shyness of cream frangipani enlivening the somewhat lifeless perfection of the rooms. When Meredith found herself becoming oppressed by the stillness, the fact that nothing was out of place, she decided that the house needed a family to fill its rooms with chatter and laughter, books and records left lying around to bring it back to life.

The kitchen was yet another surprise. Presided over by a middle-aged Chinese man whose name was Joe Kean, it was brand new.

'Mr Dane had it done,' Tafau said proudly. 'Last year. A woman came over from Australia and watched Joe for a whole week, then she sat down for another week and drew the plans. Makes cooking easier, doesn't it, Joe?'

Joe smiled. 'Yes, much easier,' he agreed, slipping an almond cookie to Mark.

Carefully overlooking this—just this once—Meredith

complimented him on the meals, received another smile and continued with her tour through the pantries and a chiller room, another guest wing decorated in somewhat faded thirties style, finally finishing out on the verandah where her grandfather was sitting in a wide cane chair, sardonically observing a tiny gecko as it made its way over his foot.

Transferring his gaze to Meredith, he barked, 'Well? Think you can do it?'

'I can learn,' she returned with dignity.

'Tafau?'

That beautiful Fijian smile appeared. 'She's got a good head on her. Don't you worry, she'll manage.'

'She'd better,' he said, still snappily. 'Come and pour the tea for me, Meredith. What will the boy have?'

'Some of that fruit juice,' said Meredith, smiling warmly at the housekeeper. 'Thank you for showing me round. Can I see you again after morning tea? There are a few things I want to ask you.'

'Yes, of course.'

When they were alone Maurice observed, 'You should be able to manage. The girls know what to do; your job will be to make sure it's done properly. Not that they need much supervision, but it's as well for them to have someone to come to when things go wrong. Joe is boss in the kitchen, of course. Don't give him orders; discuss things with him. He's a damned good cook but independent as a mule, and I don't want to lose him because you've put his back up.'

'I'll try not to,' Meredith said sweetly as she handed him his tea. A temperamental tyrant in the kitchen would enliven her life immensely.

Maurice snorted, watched Mark as he drained his glass and said abruptly, 'You'll want a nurse for him too. Ginny thinks a Karitane from New Zealand would be a good idea.'

Meredith had no idea what a Karitane was, but the fact that Ginny had suggested one was enough to make her hackles rise.

'I prefer to look after him myself,' she said primly, taking a deep breath. 'After all——'

'A Karitane nurse would take all of the responsibility from your shoulders.'

Meredith stared up at Dane, startled at his sudden appearance from behind her. Something of a jibe in his voice as he spoke made her say very firmly, 'I don't want to have the responsibility taken from my shoulders. He's had enough disturbance in the last few months. What he needs now is time to settle down and become at home here.'

The two men looked at each other, then Maurice shrugged. 'All right. In that case Renadi can be his nurse. Vasilau tells me she's very good with children, so she's the logical one. You'll need another housemaid; get Tafau to hire one. She'll know who. And listen to me, madam. You'll let Renadi look after the child; I'm not having him grow up dependent on you for his happiness.'

Meredith had poured Dane a cup of tea; for some reason she looked at him now, but his amber eyes beneath the dark straight brows revealed nothing but a bland lack of interest. Very carefully she took another deep breath, mainly to still the fluttering in her stomach. Mark, the cause of this was craning his head, chuckling to himself as he watched another gecko in the vine which overhung the verandah. He looked very small, charmingly innocent of the battle being waged over him.

'He's dependent on me for his happiness,' she said, sincerity blazing in her voice as she tried to break through her grandfather's cynicism. 'When Mother died it was the end of the only life he's ever known. I'm the only familiar thing here, apart from his toy rabbit. Give him time to settle down before you think of making any more changes.'

Maurice grunted. 'Sentimental idiocy! You're as bad as your mother, girl. Well, Dane?'

Perhaps the biggest surprise of this surprising day.

Dane said coolly, 'I think she's right. But it seems to me that you're arguing about nothing. You've agreed that Renadi should take over as his nurse; why scrap over his dependence? You can't expect him to be emotionally independent until he's considerably older.'

'Become a pediatrician?' Maurice asked scornfully, his

brows lowered to hide his eyes, one finger tapping the
arm of his chair.

Dane grinned. 'Hardly,' he returned. 'But neither am I
as stubborn as either of you.'

Astoundingly Maurice smiled. 'You call it determination, of course, and count it a virtue in yourself. Well,
miss, you can have your way. You'll continue to be responsible for the child, but Renadi will take care of him.'

Meredith felt as though somehow the ground had been
cut away from beneath her feet, leaving her outmanoeuvred and at a disadvantage. Infuriatingly, she
had no idea how this had been managed, or why; she
could only comfort herself with the determination to
make sure that whatever happened, Mark should not
suffer.

## CHAPTER FOUR

AFTER lunch everything slowed down. Mark slept, of
course, and Meredith had a strong suspicion that most of
the staff slumbered too. It was the cool season, but by
midday the sun glowed whitely in a pale sky, beating
down on to a submissive earth, and all nature needed to
rest.

Meredith showered, then occupied herself with writing
letters to friends back home before stretching out along
the chaise-longue on the verandah. Beneath her lashes the
outline of the plants shading it made green shapes against
the dazzling glare of the sky. After a while she too slept,
dropping off in the middle of wondering just how hot it
became in the summer season.

Fortunately she woke before Ginny arrived, but as
with Mark, a daytime nap tended to sour her temper.

'Come one, sweetie,' she said wearily after failing to
cheer him up. 'Let's go and have a swim. That will cool
us down.'

'Yes,' he agreed solemnly. 'And a drink, please?'

'O.K.'

'O.K.,' he mimicked, smiling at her as he raced off to find his swimsuit.

Meredith resisted the tears which threatened. He was little and gallant, and the loss of his mother had been so shattering that he still looked for her wherever he went. Hoping fervently that time would ease the aching emptiness in both their hearts, she followed him down the passage to the door which led out on to the terrace and thence to the pool.

After ten minutes she realised that they had an audience. Maurice had positioned himself under the umbrella of a shower tree, and behind him, looking rather wistful, was Renadi.

'Come on in,' Meredith called, beckoning the girl.

There was a short colloquy, Maurice nodded, then Renadi came shyly across to the edge and, still in her *sulu*, lowered herself into the water.

There followed a joyous half hour. Entranced by this girl who swam in her clothes, Mark forgot to be shy, even allowing her to take him on her back as she swam. Meredith pulled herself out of the water, warned by a tingling on her skin that she had been long enough in the sun, and walked across to her grandfather, letting the water dry on her body.

'That bathing suit is indecent,' he stated.

She grinned. 'Rubbish. It's a very restrained bikini.'

'No bikini is restrained,' he retorted. 'Have you something to put over it?'

'Yes.' The towelling jacket was too hot, but it hid everything save her long legs.

'That's better. Remember that the Fijians are an extremely modest people; it's very poor style to embarrass them.'

'Do you mean I shouldn't wear a bikini here?'

He frowned, then owned reluctantly, 'No, of course I don't, but make sure you cover yourself when you're out of the pool.' He glanced at the fine soft skin on her legs.

'Not that you'll sunbathe much if you're wise. You're too fair.'

'I'm not stupid,' she said, irritated by the way he seemed to be handing out orders all of the time.

'Time will tell. Go and tell Renadi to get changed before she takes the child back to the house. I suppose you've left his clothes there?'

Meredith bit her lip, angered yet forced to hide it. When Renadi had gone Mark played happily with a special stone he had found while Meredith and her grandfather sat in silence. But when the Fijian girl, fresh in a new gold skirt and tunic, came back she said with a note of determination in her voice, 'I'll go with them.'

'Get into a decent dress,' he said. 'Ginny is known for her taste in clothes.'

Fuming, Meredith accompanied Mark and Renadi back to the house, showered and washed her hair and picked over the dresses in her wardrobe, finally choosing a soft lilac and white sun-frock which made her eyes turn faintly purple and enhanced the soft gold of her shoulders and arms.

So it was infuriating when, out on the verandah, her grandfather looked at her from beneath his brows and said curtly, 'Ginny can take you shopping tomorrow. You'll need some better clothes than that.'

Fortunately, just in time to prevent a hot and extremely tactless reply, the elegant Miss Moore arrived on the scene, dressed superbly in a stark blue which emphasised the brilliance of her eyes and chestnut hair. With her were two people, brother and sister, by name Sarah and Peter King—New Zealanders, Ginny informed Meredith with a smile which forgave them for being born there. Sarah was home from university for the holidays, while Peter and his father worked for one of the airlines. They were twins, and twenty years old.

Meredith had to admire the gracious tact with which Ginny handed out these snippets of information, burying them in conversation designed to set them all at ease. Unfortunately her admiration didn't increase her liking for the woman at all.

But the Kings were fun, once they had forgotten their

awe of Maurice. Meredith would have liked to go away and get to know them without Ginny's oppressive presence, then told herself that it was probably her instinctive dislike of the woman which made her feel that Ginny was overdoing the good hostess act; she seemed determined to keep the conversation on an extremely tight rein as if afraid it might get out of control.

It was with a feeling of relief that Meredith saw Dane come through the doorway. Surely now Ginny would stop directing the conversation so restrictively. But no; she smiled at him with a little extra warmth and dovetailed him into the group, but that was all.

Amazing, for a woman who was supposed to be in love with him. Meredith disliked him intensely, yet she was extremely aware of him, handsome and magnetic across the table, and one glance at Sarah had revealed that she too was very conscious of his presence. Yet the woman he loved had betrayed nothing more than a mild pleasure at his arrival. Perhaps she was frigid, Meredith thought; in which case things were likely to be sticky. Dane was very much in command of himself, but there was passion in the hard mouth and if ever he relaxed his guard those tawny eyes would find it easy to blaze with emotion. Even she, inexperienced though she was, could see that.

An odd prickling of her nerves made her aware of the fact that she had been staring, and that he was watching her, his hooded eyes saturnine. As heat washed across her cheeks she turned her head away, ostensibly to watch Mark who was playing with a set of blocks which had mysteriously appeared on his bed after his swim. It took her a moment to compose herself, but she refused to allow that unnerving gaze to upset her. After all, she had been staring, her eyes lingering over his features as if she was trying to impress them on her memory. He had every reason to stare back at her. But not as if she were something amusingly repulsive from under a stone, she thought indignantly.

When the tea tray was brought out Litia set it before Meredith, who poured with as much dignity as she could muster, thinking that it should have been placed before

Ginny as she seemed to consider herself the hostess. Not by a word or the flicker of a muscle did the older woman betray emotion, but Meredith was convinced that she was angered by Litia's action. At least she stopped manipulating the conversation and leaned across to engage Dane in a low voice.

Sarah and Peter relaxed, began to suggest places for Meredith to go and things to do.

'Have you been to the Coral Coast yet?' Peter asked. 'There are some lovely places there and you travel through a quaint pine forest. The trees grow so fast that they look like those cactus things you see always with a Mexican sleeping under them.'

'Have you seen the firewalkers?' This was Sarah. 'They come from Bequa Island, on the other side. It's the most dramatic show I've ever seen! The Indians do it as part of their religious ceremonies too, but the Fijians put on shows at the hotels. You must go.' She darted a swift, sly look at her brother. 'Why don't we make up a party to go next week, Peter? Meredith would love them.'

'That's a neat idea.' He turned to Maurice. 'Could we do that, sir?'

'Meredith is old enough to accept for herself,' Maurice said bluntly, his shrewd eyes fixed on the earnest face of the young man opposite him. 'We have guests coming on Monday and Thursday, but apart from those nights she's free.'

So it was arranged, as was a trip to the club the next morning.

'Your brother will find lots of other kids to play with there,' Sarah told her. 'In the morning all the mothers hold a sort of informal kindergarten. How about having lunch there too?'

Meredith hesitated, then said, 'No, thank you. I think it would be a good idea to come home for lunch. Mark gets tired by the end of the morning.'

As if she had called him Mark came racing towards her, tripped over one of the blocks and fell, crashing into Ginny's chair. Her teacup tipped sharply, sending a wave of hot liquid over the immaculate dress.

There was a moment of silence during which Meredith quailed at the cold fury in the older woman's eyes, before Mark began to roar. Scooping him up, she tried to comfort him. Unfortunately he was inconsolable; perhaps the accumulated events of the past few days had built up tension which needed release.

When after a few moments his screaming showed no signs of abating, Meredith rose to her feet, cradling the hot little figure in her arms.

'Excuse me,' she said, aware of all the eyes on her. 'I'll take him off and calm him down.'

Her grandfather said harshly, 'Give him to Renadi.'

'He's not likely to settle with her,' she returned. 'I shouldn't be too long.'

However, it was a good twenty minutes before he sobbed himself into quietude and then he clung, limpet-like, to her, burying his face in the hollow of her shoulder.

They were sitting on the verandah when Dane appeared behind them.

'Has he recovered?' he asked.

Meredith heard the note of censure in his voice but refused to allow herself to be intimidated by it. 'Yes, he's getting better. And when Renadi has brought you some pineapple juice you'll be one hundred per cent, won't you, my darling?'

A prodigious sniff was the only reply. Meredith searched for a handkerchief, and found that Dane was beside her holding out his.

'Use it,' he said irritably when she stared at him. 'I can't abide sniffing children.'

When Mark had had his face wiped he ventured to sit up, eyeing with curiosity the man who leaned against the pillar.

'Dane,' he said proudly.

'You'd better make it Uncle Dane,' Meredith told him.

But Dane said, 'I'm not his uncle, and I refuse to be known as third cousin twice removed Dane. Let him call me what he likes.'

So beneath that chilling exterior there lurked a sense of humour. Meredith was surprised all over again, especially when Mark beamed at him as if he had known and loved him all his life.

'Dane,' he said again as he slipped from her lap and headed across the verandah. Grasping one immaculately tailored trouser leg, he said urgently, 'Come on.'

Dane lifted his brows, removed the sticky little paw but made no effort to disengage his hand when it was taken. 'Where to?' he asked.

'Mine house.' And they set off through the border of vegetation to where the little *bure* beckoned from beneath its tree, Mark's high-pitched babbling showing none of his customary shyness, occasionally interspersed with the deep, not quite so cold tones of Dane's responses.

Fanning herself with her straw hat, Meredith pursed her lips in a silent whistle. So Dane was not entirely ogreish all through. She hoped that Ginny Moore realised that it was on the cards she would be expected to have children. Try as she would, though, she could not imagine the older woman in a maternal role. She would probably hire a Karitane nurse, Meredith thought, her lip curling in spite of herself, and see her children for five minutes each day when they were on their best behaviour.

Because this sounded perilously like spite she jumped to her feet, banishing such thoughts with a sternness which said much for the basic sweetness of her character. She really must not allow Ginny Moore to bring out the worst in her, she decided, or she would begin to develop an obsession about her.

Unfortunately for this praiseworthy decision a brief knock on the door heralded the object of it.

Meredith stood, startled, in the doorway on to the verandah, her slenderness emphasised by the darkness of the foliage background. Without thinking she said, 'Goodness, I hope that tea doesn't stain! I'm sorry Mark tripped just then.'

'It was an accident,' said Ginny, her smoothly modulated voice without expression. 'Does he often have tantrums?'

Subduing the automatic bristling this evoked, Meredith replied, 'He doesn't have tantrums at all. Things just got a bit too much for him.'

'Among my relatives that sort of thing is called a tantrum,' the older woman observed dispassionately. 'I hope that isn't normal behaviour for him. If it is you'll have to make sure that he isn't present when there are guests. I doubt if Maurice will put up with screaming fits. I could see that he felt humiliated. He has very high standards, you know.'

'You must explain that to Mark,' Meredith retorted, grabbing for her temper. 'I doubt if he'll understand, and until he does Maurice—and everyone who lives here—will just have to put up with a normal small boy's perfectly normal reactions in exceptional circumstances. He's too young to be polite or hide his feelings.'

The beautifully coloured lips thinned into a straight line, but Ginny was too much in command of herself to allow anything so vulgar as anger to appear. But she was astute enough to make her emotion felt in the most ladylike manner.

'When you've been here a little longer you'll appreciate the fact that Maurice has been extremely kind to offer you a home. I don't suppose you have any idea just how important he is in the South Pacific; much more so than he was when your mother ran away. Naturally he expects everyone to measure up. He's quite ruthless enough to rid himself of anything that doesn't, you know.'

By now Meredith was so furious that it took more self-control that she knew she possessed to subdue her emotions. Indeed, she could feel a hot patch of colour on each cheek. How dare this—this *bitch* take it on herself to tell her how to behave, threaten her with dismissal as if she were an insolent servant!

With an effort to keep her voice steady she retorted, 'I've no doubt. Perhaps it hasn't occurred to you that I am a Fowler too. I could assure you that I can be every bit as ruthless as my grandfather. However, I don't consider it your business, and I doubt very much whether Maurice will, either. Had you something else to discuss with me?'

This time she had struck, home. For a moment Ginny looked as though she would like to hit her; indeed her hands clenched on to her expensive handbag for a revealing second before they were carefully relaxed.

'Yes, I have,' she said, the low voice somewhat strained. 'Maurice wishes me to choose some clothes for you. Be ready tomorrow morning at nine o'clock.' She cast a venomous look behind Meredith; Mark's voice had suddenly lifted in song. 'And don't bring him with you. He'll be a nuisance and I'm not prepared to act as a baby-sitter.'

Even though her heart sank at the prospect of going shopping with this totally unsympathetic creature, Meredith had to admit that Ginny Moore would know the best places to go. And such an expedition would be no place for Mark.

So she managed to say with as much aplomb as she could summon, 'Very well, then. I'll be ready.'

'Good.' Perhaps it was a measure of her anger that Ginny left the room with only that abrupt farewell. Normally, Meredith was sure, she would have said her goodbyes with the studied courtesy which she had displayed earlier on in the afternoon.

Meanwhile she had certainly managed to shatter any peace of mind Meredith possessed. As she pressed a cold cloth to her burning cheeks she owned that to face an enemy was a horrid experience, especially when she didn't know why Ginny Moore disliked her so intensely. Perhaps it was that instinctive hatred one read of and refused to believe in. Whatever, it was as shattering as its opposite, love at first sight, was supposed to be.

But what a nerve the woman had! To take it on herself—biting her lip, Meredith forced her thoughts away from the incident. She would not allow Ginny to upset her; indeed, if she and Dane married there must be no open breach. It would make life too awkward for everyone. But Ginny must be made to realise—forced to realise, if that was the only way—that she had no right to censure Meredith or offer threats. Perhaps a life spent without relatives had given rise to some sense of family loyalty in Meredith; she felt that she could bear Maurice's restrictions, even that Dane had some small right to comment on her behaviour. But certainly not his unofficial fiancée.

By now, thoroughly strung up, she contented herself with making a hideous face at her reflection in the mirror above the handbasin before making her way out to where Dane and Mark were.

A strange shyness held her still and quiet in the dense shade of the tree fern. Dane was standing watching Mark as he displayed his treasures, the two figures strongly contrasted, and yet the small dark boy and the tall dark man shared an unmistakable likeness. The Fowler stamp, Meredith thought wryly. It wasn't a physical thing, for they didn't resemble each other in feature at all. Dane was all hard fine lines and strength while Mark's babyish, almost cherubic expression was open and guileless. Yet they shared an animal grace which transcended the one's youth and the other's sophistication, and when an incautious movement of her hand betrayed her presence the movement of each head as it turned was identical, as was the expression on each face—alert, a little wary, yet with the kind of superb self-confidence which is usually lost before childhood has passed.

'Come and see,' Mark ordered briskly.

The sun turned her smooth wave of silken hair into a pale aureole as she approached them, moving with the kind of grace she had discerned in them both, and like them with a total lack of self-awareness. The man's glance hardened, rested with sharp assessment on her face.

'What's the matter?'

Well, she had never been one to tell tales. 'Nothing,' she evaded, bending to touch Mark's cheek, and only incidentally, she told herself, to avoid Dane's too knowledgeable gaze.

He might have believed her. Certainly he didn't pursue the subject. 'In that case I'll go,' he said indifferently. 'I've work to do.'

Mark looked up. 'Come again,' he said, smiling with an enchanting openness which made Meredith's heart contract. Don't learn to love him, she thought so vehemently that for a moment she thought she had spoken aloud.

Indeed Dane was looking at her with a cynical amusement, as though he was aware of her instinctive retreat. But he merely said, 'I'll do that,' and swung off across the grass, the light of the westering sun gilding his masculine beauty. In spite of the warmth Meredith felt her skin tighten into a shudder; for a moment she stared after him, then bent and hugged Mark, deriving comfort from his sticky kiss without asking herself why she needed it.

Perhaps to prepare herself for what came later that evening. Dane went out to dinner, so she and Maurice dined together, but he seemed gloomy and preoccupied, and after a short time spent out on the verandah he went to his room.

Meredith rang the King residence, told Sarah that she wouldn't be able to meet her at the club the next morning and made an appointment for the day following. Then she resumed her seat on the verandah, determined to catch up on some mending.

Unfortunately for such a worthy aim, the night magic made her restless; after several missed stitches she dropped the pair of shorts she was working on into her workbasket and stepped softly across to the edge of the verandah, inhaling deeply of the fragrances borne on the soft night breeze. Everything here spoke of fertility, she thought fancifully—the incredible growth, the variety, the lush vigour which the vegetation attained. And this was the dry side of the island! Even the perfumes were erotic; the heavy sweetness of the frangipani flowers ravished her senses, filling her with a soft yearning which she did not recognise.

Like a dreamy wraith she moved silently around the garden, lost in the shadows of shrubbery and pergola, picked out by the silver of the moon's rays when she walked across the grass. Other things were attracted by the night too; she could hear rustlings and scufflings in the trees and on the ground. Fiji, she knew, possessed very few snakes, so she was not afraid, although a concourse of toads on one of the lawns startled her. Fortunately they were as much afraid of her, and surprisingly nippy on their long hind legs, as she discovered when she approached one.

After a timeless interval she turned, sighing, back towards the house. Romantic surroundings had roused romantic desires within her; a racing in her blood gave rise to an urgency which half frightened her by its intensity.

So this was the spell of the tropics, she thought, trying to recapture her usual practical outlook by dissecting the sensations which held her in thrall. A combination of warmth and soft air and fecundity, a moon like a silver lantern washing the ground with silver, not the pale fairy glamour of home but something infinitely more beckoning, promising unlawful delights. On a night like this one could lose one's head and not count the cost.

Had that been what had happened to her mother? Suspended from a branch of the raintree was a swing seat, the cushions protected by a canopy from the dew which sifted through the folded leaves. It was a quaint, old-fashioned thing; perhaps Dinah Fowler had rested through the heat of the day there. Meredith climbed on to it, lying full length so that she looked up at the stars, bright diamonds against the sky.

Had Dinah fallen in love with longing and followed that deceitful moon to a life which had cut her off from all that she had ever known? How little one knew of one's mother, Meredith marvelled. Only at the end, when the barriers between the generations had been broken down by pain, had Dinah become a person in her own right, no longer the loved stay of Meredith's young life, taken entirely for granted. Had she really loved Barry Colfax, that clever, charming and totally unreliable man, or was it the effect of too many tropical nights on a lonely young girl, unable to resist the promptings of her sexuality?

Sighing once more, Meredith admitted that she would probably never know. Where Dinah could praise she had praised, remaining eloquently silent otherwise. The only person she had ever spoken hardly of was Maurice, and then she had been warning her daughter, unable to do anything else, hurt by the knowledge that both she and the little son born of that second honeymoon would be in his power.

A car swung up the driveway, the gold beams of the headlights shocking against the silver and black of the night. Outside the house the engine was cut, then a door slammed and within a few seconds the vehicle moved quietly on to the garages. Dane. By screwing up her eyes Meredith could read the face of her watch. Heavens, but it was almost midnight, and she had been mooning around for too long. Mark habitually woke at dawn and liked her to wake then too. But she decided to stay where she was until Dane had had time to get to bed. After an evening spent with the acidulous Miss Moore he would be even more judgmental than ever, and she did not want to be provoked into losing her temper once again.

A gentle movement of her legs set the seat swaying, its presence betrayed only by the slightest creak, hardly discernible above the flutterings and shufflings of the night creatures. A satellite made its way across the sky, a small lonely beacon of man's technology aping those reminders of his insignificance, the stars. Meredith felt a surging need for someone who understood her. With the still unresolved yearnings which the night had put into her blood it was a pretty heady mixture.

When Dane spoke she gave a strangled yelp, the back of one hand pressed across her mouth.

'Making eyes at the moon?' he asked with smooth insolence. 'Poor Meredith, alone and bereft.'

'Go jump off a roof!' she spluttered, furious with him for destroying her mood. 'Where are you?'

A piece of darkness detached itself from the trunk of the tree. In the subdued light he loomed over her, his expression unreadable yet close enough for her to be able to smell the faint scent of expensive cigar and something else which might have been aftershave but was far more likely to be Ginny Moore's perfume.

'I thought you were waiting for me,' he said. 'You set the swing going just as I came out on to the verandah.'

'What conceit,' she mocked, wishing fervently that he would go away before the beating of her heart overpowered her. 'I didn't even see you, and well you know it!'

There was a white flash as he smiled. 'How could I know it? It seemed a rather obvious invitation, and as I feel in a good mood I thought I'd not disappoint you. Move over.'

'No. You seem to forget that you gave me a very definite hands off signal not so long ago.' Little shocks of awareness were running through her nerves, stimulating her into vibrant alertness. Unsuspecting of the cause, she found herself speaking rapidly, almost stuttering in an effort to gloss over her physical reaction with words. 'You must be the most arrogant man I've ever met, and that includes Maurice. I don't want you near me!'

'What are you going to do about it?'

He was standing too close for her to be able to get out of the wretched swing with any degree of dignity, but she tried, swinging her legs down as she sat up.

Swift as a hawk diving on its prey, he grabbed her wrists, letting her feel his strength before seating himself beside her. When he spoke there was no mockery in the deep voice, nothing but implacable dislike, while his fingers tightened against the fragile bones.

'I want to talk to you. Are you going to stay, or do I have to force you?'

'You're hurting me!' she gasped.

'I'm enjoying it. Well?'

A bead of sweat stood out on her top lip. After a moment she swallowed and said harshly, 'I'll stay, you— you *sadist!*'

'You bring out the worst in me,' he remarked conversationally, releasing her as if her touch contaminated him.

It surprised her that he didn't wipe his fingers with the handkerchief he no doubt had at the ready.

'Well, what do you want to say?' she demanded

fiercely, glad that he had hurt her and made her angry, for it almost swamped all those peculiar sensations she had suffered when he towered over her.

'I'm aware of the fact that women like you actively resent those of your sex who provide any competition, but I told you before that I'll accept no insolence from you where Ginny is concerned. I meant it. You'll treat her with the respect she's entitled to.'

'Her estimation or mine?' she retorted savagely, rubbing her maltreated wrist against the soft curve of her breast.

'Meredith,' he said, the softness of his tones a sinister threat, 'don't make things hard for yourself. You're not stupid.'

'Look, I realise that I came here with the immense disadvantage of some independence of spirit. You and Grandfather would like a docile halfwit, but I'm not going to pretend to be something I'm not. If your lady love wants me to grovel, well, she can wait until the sky falls in for all I care! I can promise you I won't be deliberately offensive, but if I'm attacked I fight back.'

The words tumbled from her lips, bravado hiding the fact that she was afraid of him, that when he turned his head to look at her she had the cowardly desire to cringe back against the canvas of the seat.

He didn't move towards her, but she felt the looming oppression of his anger reach across the few inches that separated them. Still with that dangerous softness he said, 'It sounds reasonable, but why do you make your dislike of her so obvious?'

'Would you mind repeating the tales she told you?' She knew that she was adding fuel to the fires of his anger, but no longer cared. 'After all, not even you can expect me to defend myself when I don't even know what the charge is.'

'Let's just get one thing straight. Ginny told me no tales.'

'Oh.' She laughed with a brittle lack of amusement. 'Then you're a mind-reader, so I don't have to spell out my reasons—you can pick them up on whatever wavelength you use.'

Sickened by the dreary little scene, she sprang to her feet, intending to leave him there and then, thinking whatever he liked. After all, she cared nothing for him or his clever bride-to-be, and the sooner he realised that she refused to justify herself the better for everyone. Including the supercilious Miss Moore.

Swift as her action was, his reaction was quicker. Before she had taken one step she was jerked into stillness by an implacable hand on her shoulder, and when she twisted to free herself he caught her hand and forced it up behind her back, pulling her to rest against him.

In pain and shock she flung up her head, trying to use it as a weapon, but he jerked her wrist upwards, sending pain through her arm and shoulder. After a moment spent biting her lips to prevent any groan forcing its way through she stood head bent forward, waiting for the slightest relaxation of his grip.

'You look very innocent, very vulnerable, exposing the nape of your neck like that,' he said, contempt icing over his voice. 'Fortunately, we know better, don't we? Now, listen to me. Your only hope of getting anything like a legacy is to stay here and act like a reasonable human being. You must see that. Maurice is likely to tie up your share, but there'll be money in it for you, even so. The same applies to Mark. Believe me, if you take him away you can kiss goodbye to any hope of any money. Are you listening, Meredith?'

'I'm listening,' she said grimly; he had relaxed his hand so that she was no longer in pain, but there was no hope of freeing herself from him. He had read exactly what her intentions were and she was held against his body, tipped back so that it would take some considerable effort to regain her balance let alone run from him. Something odd happened in the pit of her stomach. Waves of sensation were emanating from there, weakening her as they bewildered her. It took a considerable amount of will-power to prevent herself from shivering like a cowed animal.

'I'm listening,' she said again, summoning up a hardness she was far from feeling, 'but you'll have to forgive me if I seem a bit startled. I thought we were discussing the elegant and non-tale-bearing Miss Moore. How did we get on to the sordid subject of money?'

'Sneering little bitch,' he stated almost without expression, turning her so abruptly that her mouth fell open in a startled O, her eyes enormous in the pale wedge of her face. 'Let's just say that one impinges on the other, shall we? Behave like a reasonable human being and you'll ultimately get what you no doubt believe to be your rights. If you don't I'll just have to get rid of you.'

'How?'

He smiled. 'Don't be silly, Meredith. Just be assured that I've the power, and the will to use it. Oh,' as he dropped her hands, 'without Mark, of course. I know he's yours and that you love him, but I think he deserves better than a childhood tied to a bad-tempered little wanton with an eye to the main chance and the morals of an alley-cat.'

If he hadn't threatened her with losing Mark she might have kept her temper. But at this she flung her head up, her eyes molten above lips white with rage.

'I hope you've quite finished,' she said, rather proud, in a disconnected way, because her voice was very level.

'I've finished.' He sounded almost bored, as though she disgusted and wearied him simultaneously.

'Good. Then *you* listen to a few home truths. I do not want anything but a home from my grandfather. I do not believe that you can separate Mark and me—the days when a woman had no rights to her children are well past, though I daresay you regret them. I have every intention of being just as polite to Miss Moore as she is to me, but I dislike being patronised by anyone. And finally, next time you come home from an evening with her find someone else to work out your frustrations on. I didn't come here to be your whipping boy.'

'Your mind obviously runs in well worn tracks,' he remarked with cold deliberation as he hauled her against him, his hand tangling in the silver gloss of her hair, holding her still with her face upturned. 'Making love might be the inevitable end to all of your evenings out, Meredith, but not mine.'

She swallowed, aware now that anger had encouraged her to say the unforgivable. Above her the dark lines of his face were deep, harshly graven, but the hand that touched her mouth and stroked the slender length of her throat was gentle.

Yet she knew that he was furiously, coldly angry and that if she moved to escape he would not care about hurting her again.

'Nothing to say?' he taunted. 'Try to look a little happier, this is what you wanted, wasn't it?'

'*No!* Dane, let me go. I don't——'

'Shut up,' he said calmly, and bent his head and kissed her.

## CHAPTER FIVE

GENTLY, as if he enjoyed the soft innocence of her mouth beneath his, and there was no anger behind the embrace. To her horror Meredith felt a thousand singing nerves leap into life, sensitising her whole body to his nearness. Dane explored her mouth with an expertise which must be partly inborn, partly the result of an immense amount of experience.

It seemed to Meredith that this was what she had been waiting for all of the long evening, this practised ravishment of her senses. For a long moment she relaxed against him, so bewildered by the unexpectedness of her response that she almost forgot the insult which had preceded the kiss. But when his hand slipped from her throat to caress the smoothness of her shoulders she stiffened, jerking her head away as she muttered a denial.

Instantly his other hand clamped tight on the hair at the back of her head, bringing sudden tears to glaze her eyes.

'Dane!' she groaned, 'for heaven's sake! Let me go.'

He smiled, but there was no humour in the movement

of his lips, none in the strangely cool glance which swept her face. 'Oh no,' he said softly. 'You're going to learn to keep your tongue under control, little cousin.'

His mouth was almost on hers; his breath warmed her skin when he spoke. Nothing she had ever experienced, no other kisses had come as close to setting her afire as this.

It must be the night and her repressed yearnings for a mate, but, dear God, it was hard to remember that this man was her enemy.

Nervously licking her lips, she demanded, 'How do you know that I won't tell Miss Moore that you think nothing of forcing yourself on me? She doesn't strike me as being particularly passionate, but I'd say she has the normal amount of possessiveness.'

'Would you?' he asked, kissing her eyelids closed with an odd smile.

Made reckless by his arrogance, she answered, 'Why not? I'll bet you'd have to do some fast talking to get yourself out of trouble, unless she's just marrying you for your money and doesn't care where or how you get your kicks.'

'What a commonplace little mind you've got,' he marvelled. 'Depressing to think that we're related, however distantly.'

Her eyes flew open, but too late. As if he avenged a thousand insults he took her mouth, forcing it open to receive a kiss unlike any she had ever experienced before, the brutal sensuality of it shocking her even as it excited her. His free hand moved to her breast, and he began to stroke and caress it rhythmically, the heat of his hand inflaming her into abandon. A hot tide of desire flooded through her body. More than anything she wanted the touch of his hands against her skin for he was driving her mad with his kiss and the caresses which opened a new world of eroticism to her.

But she knew, perhaps with the Fowler part of her brain, that although he was enjoying her he was also punishing her, and when he lifted his head she put her hand against his chest and pushed smartly, ignoring the pain as she tore her hair free from his fingers.

She whirled, poised for flight, a slender thing in a moon-silvered dress, her lips swollen beneath eyes which would have killed had they had the power. Deep breaths lifted her slight breasts, shuddered through her lips as she fought for control.

Detachedly she noted that Dane too was breathing heavily; that he watched her from beneath the straight black brows with an odd smile which made her skin prickle.

'If you ever touch me again,' she threatened after a long moment, 'so help me, I'll seduce you and tell your bitchy girl-friend every last detail!'

Even as she said them the words burnt in her brain. Dear God, how could she be so cheap and vulgar! A wave of hot colour washed over her cheeks, but she refused to reveal her shame, staring him out.

'If you end up in my bed, you'll stay there permanently,' he told her almost with indifference. 'I'll marry you and tame you, you little vixen.'

The idea of it raised the hair on the back of her neck. 'Like hell,' she retorted. 'I'd rather be your mistress than marry you, and I can think of no greater purgatory than being your mistress. You can't force me to do anything.'

'There's always Mark.' He smiled when she stiffened, and went on coolly, 'You've got courage, I'll grant you that, but you're reckless and you don't use your brain. Put one foot out of line, sweet cousin, and you'll lose everything—Mark, the money, the prestige of being Maurice Fowler's granddaughter, this home—the lot!'

The ruthlessness in his voice made her shiver. He spoke with lazy calmness, but the threat was no idle one, and when he came towards her she backed until the tree trunk stayed her, the dark pools of her eyes fixed painfully on to his face.

His hand came up and took her chin, turning it so that the moon's rays fell on to the triangular face, emphasising the high cheekbones, the delicate brows and soft mouth.

'You're out of your class,' he said, like an indulgent uncle, 'and you know it, Meredith. Why fight? It shouldn't be very hard to accept the limitations of your role here; after all, the recompense is likely to be enor-

mous. With Maurice behind you you can look forward to
a life of ease and wealth, your pick of husbands and a
future for Mark in which you'll figure largely. Bloody-
mindedness could lose you the lot.'

Mesmerised by the brilliance of his gaze, she swallowed.
Through lips which were dry with self-control she said
huskily, 'I want the best for Mark, but what I think best
isn't what Maurice wants. And you're on his side.'

'I'm on nobody's side,' he said crisply, releasing her.
'Come on, let's go up. You're cold.'

Meredith was shivering, but it was not the coolness of
the air which chilled her skin. If being close to him made
her so conscious of a weakness in her bones she was going
to have to spend her time dodging him, she thought de-
spairingly. His attack, for that was what it had been, had
opened to her a world of sensation she had never imagined. A world where the values and principles so carefully instilled by her mother had been swamped by a raw
sensuality, as primitive as it was powerful. When his hand
had closed on her breast she had felt desire like an arrow
shaft through her body, a wave of sensation which left her
stunned by its strength.

He assumed, of course, that she was as experienced as
he so obviously was, so she could not blame him for kissing her as though she was a wanton. But he had wanted
to hurt her, to force her to realise that he was stronger,
more ruthless than she and in that he had succeeded.

In a few words, the man was dangerous.

Up at the house he stopped to pour himself a small
whisky and as he topped it up with water said quietly,
'Remember what I've said, Meredith. Your only hope of
being able to influence Mark's life lies in curbing your
reckless desires and learning to behave like the sort of girl
Maurice wants you to be. Otherwise he'll send you away.
He's old enough not to care about publicity and hard
enough to cut you off without a cent.'

'I've no doubt,' she returned, 'but I'm not going to
turn into a puppet just to satisfy him. I am what I am,
and you'll all have to put up with that. As for Mark—
well, we'll see. Your threats don't frighten me.'

Even to herself her voice lacked conviction. Dane looked up and smiled with irony.

'You sound like a child defying its father. Get off to bed, Meredith. And tomorrow, be polite to Ginny.'

'Or no doubt I'll be punished again.'

His smile narrowed. 'Was it a punishment? I have the strangest conviction that you enjoyed it as much as I did.'

Meredith cast her eyes upwards. 'Such egotism! Have you always thought you were God's gift to womankind, or did it only come when Maurice chose you to be his heir?'

'Meredith,' he said, very softly, 'go to bed. Now. Without another word.'

She fled.

There ensued an uneasy period of peace which seemed to Meredith to have a waiting quality to it. Clothes were duly bought; Ginny was inclined to be icy when her recommendations were ignored, but perhaps Dane had said something to her too, for apart from a tightening of the beautifully coloured lips and a few acid comments she had made no fuss.

And the clothes certainly made a difference, Meredith decided, surveying herself in the mirror before dinner each night. Maurice seemed to have embarked on a 'meet-my-granddaughter' campaign. There were dinners, lunches, trips to the Club and several occasions when people gathered for drinks. Her possession of a wardrobe which enhanced her physical attributes gave her a confidence she would otherwise have lacked.

Meredith discovered that her ideas of life in the tropics were at a distinct variance with the truth, or perhaps it was just that Maurice insisted on a formality which was rooted in the past. Certainly things were infinitely more relaxed in the King household, with people dropping in at all hours of the day and night, impromptu parties and occasions when everyone piled into cars and went swimming in someone's pool or at one of the glorious beaches along the coast.

The Kings were fun; through them Meredith was in-

troduced to a younger set, and because they were im-
partially hospitable their callers were not limited to their
age group or that of their children. Mark, too, found
playmates there, and when Meredith took him to the
Club in the mornings he played happily with an assort-
ment of children while she and the mothers gossiped
quietly as they watched.

Yes, the clothes helped. So did the kindness everyone
showed her, and the lovely days, hot yet tempered by
breezes from the sea, and the cheerful Fijians, their
laughter as unselfconscious as their behaviour. Slowly, in-
sensibly, Meredith found that a tight coil of tension
within her was relaxing. Laughter came more readily to
her lips, the smoky circles under her eyes faded; she even
put on a few much-needed pounds.

Mark, too, blossomed, his olive skin turning to deep
golden brown as he played and swam and made the
house echo with his laughter in the long golden days. He
positively revelled in the heat and the dry calm air.

Down on the coast the sugar cane was cut, miniature
engines pulling their long trains of dusty brown canes
along the narrow railroad to the huge mill at Lautoka.
Patches of smoke by day and flame by night marked
where the fields were set on fire.

'No, not before harvesting as in Queensland,' Maurice
told her from her vantage point in the garden overlooking
the coastlands. 'We have no pests to be a hazard. The
cane is cut, fired, and then allowed to grow for another
year. After that it's replaced. Cane is like cotton, it de-
pletes the soil.'

'Have you any cane plantations?'

He shot her a swift glance from beneath his brows. 'Not
here. Almost all of the sugar on Viti Levu is produced by
Indians, descendants of the indentured labourers brought
here last century. They lease the land from the Fijians.
The firm owns a plantation on Vanua Levu, the second
biggest island, to the north of us.'

Meredith nodded. She was already familiar with the
map, marvelling at the four hundred or so islands which
made up this small country. From where she stood, in the

dense cool shade of an immense banyan, she could gaze out across the small chequer board fields to where some of those islands rested like amethysts in a green sea. They were the Mamanuca and Yasawa chains, but closer to the port of Lautoka were the resorts, little coral cays where, so Peter King had told her, the sea was a fairyland of colour and life. Further away was Hibiscus Island, the resort using up only the small part of the island which wasn't devoted to an immense copra plantation.

'Why do you live here?' she asked, made abrupt by memories of that first time she had seen Dane. 'I'd have thought that Australia or New Zealand would have been more at the heart of things.'

Her grandfather's smile was almost contemptuous. 'My great-grandfather came here from England in the days when the natives were the most feared cannibals in the South Seas. Eventually he became a trader, taking his vessel everywhere there was a profit, across to Tahiti, down to New Zealand, even up to Hawaii and the coast of California. He stole an aristocratic Spaniard from the Philippines to be his bride; in time she married him. My grandfather said that they fought like hell cats and loved like demons. When she died he followed her two days later. That's where you get your spirit. This house was started by my grandfather,' he added. 'He was one of eight children; Dane's father was another. He settled in Melbourne, in Australia. You can't go anywhere around the Pacific without meeting up with relatives. There's even a branch at Valparaiso in Chile, all languorous smiles and flashing eyes but doing very nicely, thank you. I live here because I'm a Fijian.'

And proud of it, his tone implied. Meredith nodded, startled by the knowledge of such a heritage. How tragic that her mother had felt impelled to cut herself completely off, thereby depriving her children from any knowledge of their history. Made wise by increasing maturity, she thought perhaps that it had been less painful for Dinah in her exile to suppress everything about the home where she had been born and grown up.

For no one could ever forget, she thought, her wide

dreamy gaze rapt as she looked about her. From her vantage point the ground fell away, revealing the sugar lands
sweeping down to the sea, their dryness broken only by
wriggly green snakes of vegetation which marked the
streams. Lautoks lay spread beneath the sun, a small,
immensely attractive town behind the port where the
sugar freighters collected their sweet cargo to carry off
around the world. A little to the south was Nadi, service
town for the international airport and the hotels which
sheltered most travellers on their first night in these enchanted isles. Beyond that was more sugar and more
spacious, beautiful beaches, pine forests and resorts.

And behind again were the mountains, great purple
cliffs raised from the depths of the earth by some cataclysmic past, the volcanic crags almost smothered by lush
tropical growth. So much beauty of form and colour
ravished the senses; with a gesture that escaped being
affectation because of its naturalness Meredith embraced
the smoothness of the tree trunk, resting her cheek against
it in an access of pleasure.

'I wouldn't leave here, either,' she said, half below her
breath. 'It's like Eden.'

And like Eden there were flaws, the biggest being the
resident beast of prey, dear cousin Dane. Not that she saw
much of him now. He escorted Ginny to various functions
in the evening, played host with superb skill when Maurice entertained and made up for lost time by eating
breakfast at some ungodly hour well before she and Mark
appeared.

Towards Meredith he behaved with an impeccable
courtesy which she might have taken at face value had it
not been for the cool irony rarely absent from his glance.
Whenever those brilliant eyes moved her way Meredith
felt again that strange animal reaction he had evoked so
effortlessly from her, but she refused to allow him to affect
her behaviour. That would be allotting him too much
importance. After all, physical attraction was merely a
kind of chemistry and no respecter of persons. He might
have the power to set her body on fire, but it meant
nothing.

Days slid into weeks, the land became drier beneath the baking sun, although in the cool evenings Meredith sometimes needed a light wrap. A sprinkler system kept the garden green and lush, giving toads and geckos the conditions they loved. Mark learnt new words, a dozen a day it seemed, and Meredith bought a camera and discovered in herself an ability to take pleasing photographs.

'You have an eye for design,' Dane commented one night after glancing over the latest batch.

Meredith felt an absurd pleasure. 'I used to sketch and paint,' she said, 'but I got so cross because I could never achieve the effects I wanted. I hadn't the talent.'

Maurice grunted, but she could see that he was not averse to her having a talent, even if a very minor one. Thick forefinger stabbing a shot of Mark, he said almost harshly, 'If you want to learn how to develop them, tell me. A friend of mine owns a print shop in Suva.'

Meredith would have liked very much to learn how to develop, but her life was full enough now without adding to it.

'Later,' she said. 'At the moment I'm still finding my way about the house. Tafau was an extremely good trainer, but looking after a place this size is quite a hectic business.'

'Finding it too much?'

It was her grandfather who spoke, but both men eyed her with the same look, a nicely compounded blend of cynicism and scorn.

'No,' she returned promptly. 'What an unflattering estimation you both have of my powers!'

Maurice smiled, shooting a swift glance at Dane. 'You certainly look as if the place agrees with you. When you arrived you resembled a plucked chicken, scrawny and pale.'

'My looks, too,' she said mournfully, before breaking out into laughter which won an answering smile from both men.

Thinking that when that hateful mockery was absent Dane was inordinately attractive, and suppressing the thrill which fired her nerves at the thought of it, she scooped up her photographs and left them.

Back in her room she listened with a half smile to Mark as he and Renadi played in the walled garden. That was one relationship which had everything going for it. Mark and his Nandi, as he called her, had become almost inseparable, their laughter mingling as they made their way about the house and grounds.

At first Meredith had worried, for Renadi seemed scarcely more than a schoolgirl herself, far too young to be responsible for a child. But she took her duties seriously, her wide brown gaze seldom removed from her small charge, and the soft voice could harden into a very convincing command when it was necessary. Meredith had to chide herself for feeling a few tinges of jealousy at Mark's prompt affection for his nurse, a jealousy assuaged by the fact that at bedtime it was his sister he wanted to read him his story and chant the nursery rhymes he loved and was now learning parrot fashion from her.

Looking after the house was hard work in one way, for her total inexperience made her far too conscientious. But the staff knew their jobs and when she admitted her lack of knowledge they helped her with such charming enthusiasm that she was almost overwhelmed by it. After a while she began to get into the swing of things, relieved to find that like all well oiled machinery, the place ran smoothly most of the time. As Maurice had said, it really only needed supervision.

Even Joe, the cook, of whom she had been slightly afraid, proved a lamb. A somewhat inscrutable one, but very lamblike, even to the extent of letting Mark play with small scraps of pastry and bread dough when approached in the right manner—the right manner being Mark's habit of bouncing into the kitchen embracing with impartiality everyone who happened to be there and then making his needs known. It worked every time. Lucky Mark!

He appeared to have even made a conquest of his grandfather. Not that Maurice showed any signs of growing fond of the child, but Meredith noted that he frequently looked for Mark when he was absent and was often to be found sitting near his grandson as he played the interminable games of childhood.

Looking back, she thought that it was probably the episode of the tree which won Maurice's respect. A short distance from the swimming pool there was a *uto* or breadfruit tree, its divided leaves like hands around the knobbly fruit, with a splendid forked trunk. Ideal for climbing, if you were two. Mark had slowly made his way across to it, and then, under Meredith's eye, proceeded to clamber carefully up, his fixed smile denoting his determination to reach whatever goal he had set himself.

At last he called out, but as he did so his grip failed him and he fell, landing in a startled heap on the coarse grass. He bellowed, of course, but quietened almost immediately.

'Never mind,' Meredith comforted him when she picked him up, 'never mind, darling, you climbed such a long way.'

She had expected him to give up, but he had allowed himself to be wiped down and then, with a bright challenging look, which for a moment gave him a startling resemblance to Dane, began once more to clamber up the tree. Meredith stayed where she was, only to be told in a peremptory fashion which reminded her even more of Dane, to go away.

So she made her way back to the chair, to find Maurice smiling somewhat grimly as he watched his grandson inch back up the tree.

This time he didn't fall, and everyone, including Matiu the gardener and Vasilau, who had come out in his unobtrusive way, cheered and told him how clever he was.

At the time Meredith thought little of it, but when she went to dinner that night Maurice was telling Dane about it, smiling with more real amusement than he had ever shown before.

'Arrogant little chap,' he said, a hint of pride in his tones. 'Ordered Meredith away and got there, then insisted on making his own way down again. Reminded me of you when you were a child.'

Dane grinned as he poured Meredith a concoction of

mango juice and ice and lemonade. 'I can't recollect ever being arrogant,' he said, narrowed eyes daring her to comment. 'High-spirited, perhaps, but surely not arrogant?'

'Perhaps it came with age,' Meredith observed sweetly.

Maurice gave a bark of laughter. 'Well, Dane?'

'If I am arrogant, which I deny, then I learnt it from a master,' he returned smoothly.

'Oh!' Meredith gave an elaborate sigh. 'How unfair to blame Maurice, who everyone knows to have a temper like honey.'

For a moment she thought that, led on by their unusual mildness, she had gone too far, but beneath their formidable exteriors both men possessed a sense of humour. Maurice gave another crack of laughter, saying with irony, 'I must be mellowing with age, God help me.'

'God help us all,' Dane agreed, lifting his glass in salute to the old man, his glance wryly affectionate. 'I'm not going to bank on it, however. You've terrorised the Pacific all your life; I hope you continue to do so until your death.'

'A fine toast.' Maurice spoke scoffingly, but there was a fierce pride in his voice which he couldn't hide as he looked at his heir. 'Do you know why I chose Dane?' he demanded of Meredith.

Considerably startled, she shook her head, repressing several excellent suggestions.

'Because he was the only man I could find who was prepared to stand up to me,' Maurice told her flatly. 'The world is full of yes-men, compliant and eager, without a creative idea in their heads. Good for most jobs, but not head of Fowlers. Dane's prepared to fight for what he wants.'

'How—elevating,' said Meredith, noting that Dane seemed not at all embarrassed by what was evidently high praise. Of course his self-assurance was the bred-in-the-bone kind, so deeply ingrained that nothing would ever affect it.

Infuriating, but not a man to be trifled with, as she had discovered. Unconsciously her finger touched her mouth;

for a moment his eyes rested on it and she looked away, raising the fragile barrier of her glass between them. He looked devastating, the gleam of the lamps emphasising the hawkish features as he began to speak to Maurice about some aspect of the business.

Meredith found herself growing interested as he discussed the terms of a contract the firm was negotiating in Indonesia. The deep clipped voice uttered no surplus word, incisively setting out the bare bones of the document, assessing, rejecting, and all with a grasp of essentials and the foresight which revealed brilliance. As she listened Meredith felt the dawning of a new kind of respect, for both Dane and her grandfather revealed themselves to be a far cry from the caricatures of greedy industrialists. They were buccaneer types, but without the rapacity of pirates; with a social conscience, in fact.

The rest of the evening passed in similar mellow fashion. Almost Meredith managed to banish the memory of Dane's kisses. Especially as he continued to treat her with an aloof courtesy which forbade any familiarity.

Perhaps, she thought wisely, he too was trying to forget that he had ever been goaded into losing control of himself. He had called her reckless, but there had been more than a touch of rashness in the passion she had roused in him. Beneath the desire to punish her had been a savage need to purge himself of appetites he despised. The violence she sensed frightened her, but she was forced to admit that his passion had evoked a response almost blinding in its intensity. He had kissed her as though she was an experienced woman; it shamed her to realise that she would like nothing better than to gain such experience with him.

But that sensible part of her brain, the Fowler part, warned her that she was responding only to the physical magnetism of the man, as did all women to a greater or lesser degree. The real Dane, the man as opposed to the sensual animal, was hard and ruthless, without tenderness, and she had better believe it. No doubt he would be a superb lover with a technique shaped to win a shattering response from women, but there was more to love than the mastery of a skill.

A sobering thought, but it did not prevent the tell-tale pulse in her throat from beating faster whenever they were in the same room together.

## CHAPTER SIX

THE Club was housed in an elegant stone building set in grounds where huge shovel-shaped leaves of Devil's Ivy scrambled in gold and green profusion up the trunks of banyans and raintrees. It was gracious and mature, built in the days when the only air conditioning was that achieved by siting and building techniques. So there were large stone verandahs to shade the windows, a multitude of creepers, dim, cool rooms with enormous electric fans hanging from the high ceilings and an air of pleasant relaxation in spite of the fact that the squash and tennis courts were the scene of frantic activity for most of the day.

Meredith enjoyed going there very much, especially the morning sessions when the place resembled a nursery school with small children swimming and playing while their mothers sat around in the shade of the mango trees and gossiped, or wrote letters, or read magazines.

Afternoons and evenings were devoted to adults; once Meredith had been with the Kings to a dance and often she played tennis or pool there, but tonight was a special occasion, the anniversary of the founding of the Club, and so this was a ball. Even Maurice was going. Dane was taking Ginny, of course; she and her mother as well as a Mr Sanders who was Mrs Moore's escort, had dined at the house, and Meredith was to be escorted by Peter who had also dined, somewhat subdued by the formality of Maurice's table, but cheering up rapidly when it became apparent that neither Dane nor Maurice were about to deliver any blighting set downs in his direction.

'You'll come in my car,' Maurice said to Peter after dinner. 'You can pick yours up after the ball.' He smiled ironically at Peter's crestfallen expression. 'Joseph will bring the car back after I've come home. I don't expect to stay for the whole evening, but I'm sure that Meredith will.'

'Thank you very much, sir.' Peter tried very hard to sound as if he meant it.

Meredith lowered her lashes, thinking that he was very young, very easy to read. Compared to Dane and her grandfather he almost seemed newly hatched, yet he was great fun and not, as were several other young men, too much in awe of the Fowler name to invite her out. But it was probably that very name which ensured that he made no demands on her, not even a kiss at the end of an evening together.

As she turned she felt Ginny's eyes on her, disparaging and very cool. A sudden prickle of antagonism lifted her head. It was not her fault that Maurice insisted she be his hostess and she was not going to let Ginny make her feel like an interloper just because the older woman fancied herself in that role.

At least she couldn't complain about her dress, she thought defiantly, welcoming the heaviness of the crêpe de chine as it swirled around her ankles, the richness of the cloth making her skin and hair glow against its dark blue colouring. Ginny had thought it too old, but Meredith knew that the straight lines emphasised the slender grace of her body, lending her height and, with any luck, a modicum of dignity.

Before dinner her grandfather had given her a pendant on a silver chain, a sapphire set in diamonds which hung invitingly just above the shadowed cleft of her breasts.

'It was my wife's,' he said, adding gruffly, 'Make sure you don't lose it.'

'Are you certain you want me to wear it?'

'Of course I am,' he retorted irascibly. 'Go on, off you go. Is the boy asleep?'

'Sound asleep.' Driven by a sudden impulse she bent, kissed his cheek, then fled without waiting for his reaction. She rather thought that he was learning to like her, in spite of the fact that he believed her Mark's mother. She hoped so, for she found in herself an affection for him. Tough as nails he undoubtedly was, but he had loved his wife, and he loved Mark.

On the way down to the Club he was silent, but as the car drew up outside the main entrance he said in his normal curt manner, 'You look very attractive tonight, Meredith. Enjoy yourself.'

Long hours of the preceding few weeks had been filled with feminine discussions about what to wear to the Ball, so Meredith was prepared for the butterfly effect of the women in the ballroom wonderfully contrasted with the men's evening attire, but the decorations made her eyes widen in delighted surprise. A dedicated committee had turned the rooms into forested glades. There were tree ferns, orchids and hibiscus, a pool and waterfall with mossy stones in one room, the ceilings transformed into a canopy of branches with lights peeping through, the walls arranged to form grottos festooned with allamanda and bougainvillea. And everywhere the perfume of gardenia and frangipani.

'It's beautiful,' she exclaimed, half bewildered by the transformation.

Maurice smiled somewhat sourly. 'There's an excellent committee in charge, but I'm afraid they are not particularly creative. They've decorated it like this for the past five years. Come and meet the president.'

Unsurprised at Dane's presence in the receiving line just within the front entrance, she looked in vain for Ginny. So their names were not that inextricably linked! Otherwise Ginny certainly would have been there with him, at her most gracious.

Lord, Meredith thought, I'm getting paranoid about the woman! Dismissing her from her mind she gave Dane a radiant smile which won an answering gleam of amusement and uplifted by a sudden flame of pleasure, accompanied Maurice to where a group of his cronies stood, glasses in hands as they watched and talked.

Some of them she knew for they had been guests at

dinner. Those who were strangers to her were introduced by Maurice. They were old hands, their faces burned dark by years spent under a tropical sun, their eyes shrewd as they summed up their old friend's granddaughter. Many would have known her mother, but her name was not mentioned; instead they greeted her with an avuncular courtesy which held no criticism but considerable interest.

Rapidly but not unkindly Maurice sent Peter away, promising to restore Meredith in time for the dancing, and proceeded to make her position obvious to those who looked on. After ten minutes no one at the club could have failed to know that she was a Fowler, and therefore entitled to respect. One of Maurice's cronies introduced her to his son, an elegant young man who almost managed to hide his alert interest in all that he thought she represented beneath an air of sophistication.

Pseudo-sophistication, for Dane joined them then and it was easy to see just who the young man had chosen for his model, and how far short he had fallen of his goal. Dislike him as intensely as she did, Meredith had to own her very distant cousin made every other man in the place seem pale and effete, lacking in charisma and vitality.

'Don't look so pensive,' he said in her ear. 'You'll upset your ageing admirers.'

Stung by the mockery in his tones she flashed him another brilliant smile, banishing the hint of thoughtfulness from her expression. It was not difficult to sparkle in such surroundings and after the first few minutes her companions had given up any hint of patronage in their attitudes to speak to her as an equal.

At last Maurice said, 'Dane, take Meredith away and deliver her to her partner, will you? She doesn't want to be stuck with a parcel of old fogies all night.'

Which was not exactly true. Peter and his friends were fun, but she had enjoyed matching wits with her grandfather's age group.

However she allowed Dane to escort her towards the ballroom feeling, in spite of her better instincts, a low kind of pride at being in the company of by far the most exciting man at the event.

Unfortunately for the success of the evening Dane said, 'Now, where's young King?'

'Over with his family, see, by the waterfall.'

'We'll collect him on the way,' he said.

'On the way?'

'Yes.' He looked down into her surprised face and smiled, the mockery intensified. 'You're in my party tonight, sweet coz.'

For some reason heat flamed across her cheeks. 'Don't *call* me that,' she retorted angrily.

'But you are sweet, as sweet as honey. You had all Maurice's friends polishing up a gallantry that hasn't seen the light of day for years.' He laughed softly at her outraged expression, touching her cheek with a hand which lingered against the smooth skin. 'And you are my cousin, aren't you?'

Defiantly she stared at him, daring him to continue. 'It might be just as well to remember that.'

'Oh, I do,' he returned blandly, taking her elbow and turning her, 'But aren't we lucky the relationship is so distant?'

Meredith found herself with no answer to this. It was hard to acquit him of the desire to flirt with her, but she did; Dane disliked her too much to indulge in light-hearted badinage. And that was a singularly enigmatic smile he bestowed on her, as if thinking things far beyond her comprehension.

A subtle tension communicated itself to her nerves, widening the pupils of her eyes so that they appeared darker, like slumbrous smoky pools in the pointed wedge of her face. Deep within her bones there was a strange ache, a kind of excitement which communicated itself by a faint flush across her cheekbones, a slightly febrile gaiety. She waited for something to happen.

The look she received from Ginny Moore should have dampened down her excitement; it was quite clear that her arrival with Dane was not at all to that one's liking, even with Peter as chaperone.

Smiling sympathetically at Dane the older woman asked, 'All the formalities over? Mr Sanders was telling us that you will be president next year, as dear old Rolly Hargreaves is retiring.' At last! her tone intimated.

'Perhaps.' Not to be drawn he steered the conversation away into other channels.

Ginny of course picked up her cue from him, being gracious to Peter and charmingly deferential to Maurice when he arrived, while her mother looked on with subdued pride.

Surprisingly enough Meredith enjoyed herself. If she would have preferred to be with the Kings no one except Dane realised it, and within a few minutes her high spirits and readiness to be entertained cast a glow over the evening. There was incessant to-ing and fro-ing between the various tables; couples came up to pay their respects to Maurice and Dane and stayed to be introduced.

Names buzzed in Meredith's ears, were banished by others, and yet more, until she was convinced that she had been introduced to everyone who was anyone on the dry side of the island.

It was exciting to whirl on the dance floor beneath the dimmed lights, exciting to listen to the laughter and chatter, to know that others were enjoying themselves just as she was. She blossomed into a beauty at once mysterious and beckoning, the deep blue of her gown emphasising the fragility of her slender swaying body, deepening the colour of her eyes so that they dominated the faintly sun-kissed triangle of her face.

Sparkling, she accepted compliments, disbelieving all but the least extravagant as she parried them.

Then, a couple of dances before supper, Dane swept her on to the floor and suddenly her excitement peaked, bloomed into a flower of such dark fascination that his eyes narrowed as he gazed down at her.

'What about Ginny?' she asked.

'She's dancing with Sanders. Her mother is talking to Maurice. And young King is about to ask someone at his parents' table. So you needn't worry about him or Ginny.'

Meredith couldn't go on staring at him with devouring eyes so she turned her head away. But that brought her cheek in too close contact with his lapel for comfort.

A sharp stab of sensation lanced through her body. In as tart a voice as she could produce she said, 'There was really no need to do this, you know.'

'And have everyone think that we don't get on?' he asked coldly. 'Have some common sense, Meredith.'

So that was it. Unaccountably her heart lurched in pain. 'How careful you are,' she marvelled, hitting out at him the only way she could.

'More careful than you, you exasperating child.'

'What have I done now?' she asked pertly. 'I've been on my best behaviour, I'll have you know.'

'Indeed? Then it's as well you've somebody here to watch your interests. Young King is well on the way to losing his head and you've set out to deliberately dazzle everyone in sight.'

'Except you,' she retorted, a queer kind of desolation encasing her heart in ice.

'Ah, but I don't count.'

Before she could repent she lifted her head, staring him straight in the face. 'Well, I don't know about that,' she murmured outrageously. 'You'd be a real challenge; and how gratifying to my ego if I brought you to your knees.'

Something frightening glittered in the back of his eyes but his expression was impassive as he taunted softly, 'You've an ego the size of a house already, darling. Cast your mind back to the only time I've touched you; I frightened the hell out of you, and that was a mere kiss. If I made love to you you'd regret the day you ever saw Fiji. I'm not an adolescent, fumbling with forces barely understood.'

The reference to Mark's supposed father made her stiffen. 'How dare you!' she breathed, furiously angry with him and with herself for precipitating this.

He laughed. 'I dare anything,' he said calmly. 'Don't provoke me.'

'I hate you!'

'Quite possibly, but you're attracted as well. Fortunately I'm not interested in nubile adolescents, however prettily packaged. Relax, will you? I object to dancing with someone who's doing a very convincing imitation of a poker.'

'How can I relax?' she demanded, apalled at the fact that he had divined her secret before she had even realised it herself, humiliated and sickened by his bluntness. Perhaps had she not claimed to be Mark's mother he might have been more gentle with her, but she could not find it in herself to be at all repentant. Mark's welfare was more important than anything. Attraction was a common thing; at least she wouldn't fall in love with him, knowing the devil behind the handsome mask.

'Deep breathing is supposed to be an excellent relaxant,' he offered with cutting politeness. 'It might look a little odd, but you could try it.'

The idea struck her as so amusing that she gave a quick gurgle of laughter.

'That's better,' he encouraged blandly. 'What a small waist you have.'

'I beg your pardon?'

'You heard. A thoroughbred, aren't you? Delicately curved virginal breasts, slender waist, narrow hips above long legs.'

Colour flooded her skin. 'What—what on earth are you getting at?' she asked unevenly.

His glance was razor-sharp. 'You blush so easily, too. Very young, very innocent. Not at all matronly.'

'I'm only nineteen,' she pointed out in her crispest tones, grabbing desperately for conviction. He could not be allowed to become at all suspicious, or he would start enquiries and she had no illusions about the success of her deception if anybody started snooping. 'Don't tell me,' she resumed, infusing scorn into her voice, 'that you're one of those men who believe that they can tell at a glance whether a woman is a virgin or not!'

He was not sidetracked. 'Hardly, my dear, but you must admit that childbearing seems to have done nothing at all to your body. I've seen you in a bikini and there are certainly none of the outward signs of motherhood.'

'Not everyone has stretch marks,' she jerked out, adding with an attempt at lightness, 'Fortunately I haven't. What are you implying, Dane?'

'Nothing,' he said, that glance still raking her features. 'Are you feeling well? You've gone a bit pale.'

'Not surprising, as you've seen fit to insult me and then try to rattle me by making stupid comments about my figure.' More than anything she wanted to go back to the table, but to say so would arouse the very suspicions she was trying to stifle. Attack was the best form of defence, she decided, saying aloud, 'What *were* you getting at, Dane?'

'Merely admiring your figure,' he returned, smiling with infuriating composure. 'A word of advice, however.'

During the pause that followed she looked at him with painful intensity, forcing herself to meet the cool deliberation of his expression with a calm questioning glance.

'Be a sensible girl,' he advised, 'and don't live in Peter King's pocket. He's half way to falling in love with you, but Maurice would have a fit at the thought of any marriage.'

'Peter's a dear,' she said fiercely.

'Of course he is, but not a suitable husband for you.'

'Any suitable husband is going to have to accept Mark,' she observed drily. 'That rather narrows the field.'

He smiled at that, such cynical appreciation in the movement of his mouth that she was repelled. 'Perhaps, my dear, but no doubt what Maurice leaves you will coat the pill.'

'You mean I'd be married for my money.'

Beneath her hand she felt the powerful shoulders lift in a shrug. 'Hardly. There are other things to take into consideration. You're a beauty and you have any number of feminine attributes. Even if you have been rather—generous—in your use of them.'

'My God, damning with faint praise indeed! I don't think I'd want to marry anyone who sees me as a meal ticket.'

'But as you pointed out only a moment ago, your choice may not be all that wide.'

It was hopeless to try and best him, although crossing swords with him had its own exhilarating effect on her mood.

'You're impossible!' she said at last, determined to overcome the fascination she felt for him before it became an obsession.

He smiled at that, grimly yet with humour. 'Perhaps it runs in the family, Meredith, for I've no doubt Maurice has heard that more times than you could count, and to my mind there's no doubt but that you're a chip off any number of old blocks.'

'That doesn't sound as if it's a compliment.'

'Far from it,' Dane agreed drily.

Disguising hurt with a fine show of anger, she flashed, 'I suppose you think women should be meek and docile, content to sit at home and come to life only when a man comes anywhere near!'

'Suppose what you like,' he said indifferently as his hand tightened momentarily but with cruel force. 'I've no interest in your opinion of me.'

'And I none in yours,' she retorted furiously.

He laughed, his expression all sardonic appreciation as he looked down into the mutinous face she lifted to him. 'Yes you have, sweetheart. You'd like to see me on my knees before you so that you'd have the pleasure of kicking me in the teeth. Well, dream your childish little dreams, but don't expect real life to be anything like them. I find you entertaining, but I'm far too wary to be snared by such obvious and well-used charms.'

'I think you're sweet, too,' she returned, only the severest self-discipline enabling her to maintain some sort of composure in the face of such brutal frankness. She even managed to smile at Peter, who was enjoying himself immensely with one of his sister's friends, transferring the smile after a few moments to Ginny Moore.

Not for the world would she reveal to that one just how much she was hurt!

Unfortunately it was very shortly after she had regained her freedom from his arms that Ginny managed to antagonise her once more. Waiting until the men were away during a lull in the dancing, she leaned across to Meredith, saying, 'You look somewhat heated, Meredith. Have you quarrelled with Dane again?'

No one appeared to be listening, although Meredith was quite sure that Mrs Moore's air of vagueness hid a very acute pair of ears.

'No,' she answered. 'We don't quarrel. Spar would be a better word, I think.'

The older woman lifted her brows. 'Don't you think you're a little foolish to annoy him? After all, he has the power to make your life highly unpleasant. I'm sure you realise that now that he controls Fowlers it's up to him whether or not you do well from the estate.'

'What estate?' Meredith was deliberately obtuse.

A faint frown appeared between Ginny's immaculately plucked brows. 'Why, Maurice's, of course.'

'But Maurice is still very much alive!'

'He's an old man, Meredith, over eighty, as I'm sure you know. You are aware, I hope, that he handed the firm—everything in fact—over to Dane some years back. So sensible of him, when he felt his powers failing.'

Meredith knew nothing whatsoever of the disposition of her grandfather's interests in the firm, but she was beginning to know her grandfather, and if he felt any failure of his powers he had certainly given no indication of it. Of course Dane must own an equity in the business. Maurice was hard, but he reposed complete and well-deserved trust in his chosen heir. But Dane had made it quite clear that her grandfather was in a position to leave her enough money to keep both her and Mark wealthy for the rest of their lives. And she preferred to believe Dane, who was cruel but possessed of a kind of rock-hard honesty which was so obvious she took it for granted, rather than Ginny Moore, who had heaven knows what axes to grind.

'Very sensible of him,' she agreed woodenly, her dislike of the woman increasing.

'Then don't you think you're being foolish—to quarrel with Dane?'

Just what Ginny was up to Meredith didn't know, but she retorted lightly, 'Ah, but I think it's good for him, don't you? He seems to be getting a little set in his ways, almost middle-aged in outlook, and I know for a fact that he isn't thirty yet. A few fireworks now and then might help to liven him up.' The devil within her impelled her to add, 'Think of it as my wedding present to you. If he always gets his own way he'll turn into a tyrant, and I'm sure you wouldn't want that.'

Lips drawn into a tight, ugly line, Ginny leant forward and said half under her breath, 'Just leave him alone, you insolent little——' For a moment she paused, obviously substituting another word for the one which had immediately come to mind, '—little *baggage!*' she finished, her glance suddenly green with malice. 'He finds you boring and your efforts to attract his attention irritating.'

With an effort so immense that it was visible, and perhaps in obedience to a swift sideways look from her mother, Ginny regained control of herself, slipping once more into the role of ever-gracious woman of the world. 'I had hoped to keep this from degenerating into a slanging match,' she said after a moment. 'But I can see that you have no idea of how to behave, another thing that disgusts Dane. He's so incredibly fastidious himself that anything the least bit crude grates unbearably. However, even that wouldn't matter if you restrained yourself from making these pathetic attempts to attract his attention. He is your cousin, after all.'

'I never forget it,' Meredith returned flippantly. For the life of her she didn't know how to cope with a situation like this, but at least until she got home the rank taste of disillusionment would have to be disguised. So Dane discussed her with Ginny, did he? For a moment she trembled on the brink of informing her antagonist of that searing kiss, but her basic common sense came to her aid. It would score off Ginny, but Dane would see to it that there was more humiliation in store for her as the tale-bearer. Lowering her head, she sipped at the fruit punch to ease a throat suddenly dry.

'Then remember that Dane has very definite ideas on relatives marrying.' Ginny hammered home her point with a bluntness which showed that she had jettisoned any ideas of finesse. 'And give up any ideas you may have formulated on that subject.'

Meredith could take no more. Rising with a suddenness which brought Mrs Moore's face around so swiftly it was clear that she had been listening all the time, she countered with a dignity which sat easily on her slender shoulders, 'Believe it or not, but such a thought never entered my mind. Now, I've had enough of this. You may get your kicks this way, Miss Moore. My tastes are less complex.'

Making her way to where Peter stood talking to a group of friends, she slipped her hand over his arm; he moved to make room for her and for the rest of that evening she took good care not to be alone with either Ginny Moore or her mother.

No one was gayer, no one more appreciative of the delights of the evening than she, and when in the early hours of the morning it was decided to watch the sunrise at a beach she agreed.

Unfortunately as they made their way out of the Club they met Ginny and Dane. Mrs Moore and her escort had already left, as had most of the older members, but it was a malignant fate which led to Dane's presence there just as they were about to leave.

Another stroke of that same evil fate was Sarah King's cheerful greeting. 'Hi, Miss Moore. Hi, Mr Fowler. Hasn't it been a super, super evening!'

Ginny was no more than gracious, but Dane gave Sarah a smile which visibly set her back on her heels. Impotently watching the effect that he had on poor susceptible members of her sex, Meredith tried to look inconspicuous, for she had a sudden feeling that Dane would not approve of their decision to go on to the beach.

'Oh, we're not going home yet,' Sarah told him blithely in answer to some comment. 'We're off to Natadola Beach for a swim. It's too lovely a night to waste sleeping.'

'Indeed?' Dane said blandly.

And that seemed to be that. But as they walked down the steps Meredith felt the back of her neck prickle.

Sure enough from just behind her, Dane said, 'I hope you weren't intending to take Meredith to the beach, Peter.'

Peter turned, answering with the wariness which the older man always evoked in him. 'Er . . . yes, I was, as a matter of fact, sir. Do—do you think Mr Fowler would disapprove?'

Fuming, because he recognised Dane's authority and gave in to it, Meredith stood still, her head lowered so that no one could see her chagrin.

'I'm certain he would,' Dane told him calmly. 'Were you planning to take Joseph?'

Peter looked dismayed. 'Oh, no, no.' He darted a harassed look at his partner. 'You sent him home, didn't you, Meredith?'

'Some hours ago,' she agreed coldly.

'In that case you can come home with me,' Dane told her, ignoring alike Ginny's sudden savage intake of breath and Peter's worried frown.

It was Peter who spoke first, obviously taken aback, but with commendable courage in the face of Dane's icy disapproval.

'I'll go with you,' he said. 'I'm not that keen on the other.'

And so it was decided. Mortified yet totally unable to influence the course of events, Meredith allowed herself to be ushered into the back seat of Dane's luxurious car, and sat, a seething witness to a conversation of such inanity between Peter and Ginny that normally she would have found it inexpressibly amusing.

Dane drove, speaking little, to the street where Ginny and her mother occupied a pretty unit. Once there he stayed for no longer than five minutes before returning. Hardly a passionate leavetaking—long enough for a swift kiss, and that was all.

'Enjoy yourself, Meredith?' he asked as he set the car in motion once more.

'Very much, thank you,' she replied, her voice expressionless.

Peter took her clenched fist, straightened out the taut fingers and squeezed them. Grateful for the warmth and unspoken message, she returned the pressure.

'You seem rather silent,' Dane probed, once more on the attack.

She wouldn't give him the pleasure of hearing her plead tiredness. 'I'm so sorry,' she said politely.

After which conversation lapsed until Dane stopped the car at the front door of the house. 'I see your car has been left ready for you, Peter,' he observed. 'Have you a key, Meredith?'

'Yes, thank you.'

'Then I'll see you in a few minutes.'

It was only when the car engine had died away that Peter spoke. 'Whew!' he muttered, grabbing her hand to pull her across the drive to where his car waited beneath the bare branches of a poinciana. '*Not* the year's brightest idea, I gather. Sorry about that, Meredith.'

'Oh, don't worry. You go with the others, though.'

'Actually, I might. Lord, he can come the old-fashioned, can't he? What did he think we were going to do, hold a drunken orgy on the beach?'

The idea was ludicrous enough to make Meredith laugh. At the sound Peter bent and kissed her swiftly, saying after a moment, 'I thought you were frightened or something, you've been so quiet.'

The kiss was inexpert, but his niceness was so welcome that she clung, breathing, 'Of Dane? Don't be a twit! I wouldn't have taken any notice of him, only I have a feeling that Grandfather wouldn't approve either. And I didn't want to give my dear cousin's arctic girl-friend the pleasure of crowing loudly.'

'Well, you've more courage than I have if you can ignore him,' he said, not at all facetiously. 'Quite frankly, he frightens the liver out of me. I always get this feeling of leashed power, as though if you made him mad he could lower the shutters and blast you out of existence. I can't think of anyone I'd rather not have as an enemy, except perhaps Maurice. They're two of a kind, aren't they?'

'You've an imagination and a half,' Meredith retorted lightly, releasing herself from his embrace. 'Go on, off you go. Goodnight—and thank you so much for a lovely, lovely evening.'

So warm was her smile that he failed to notice the throb of emotion in her voice.

'It's been a lovely night for me, too,' he said, adding impulsively, 'You're such a sweet thing, Meredith. Good-night.'

Slowly she walked back up the steps to the verandah. Now that the necessity for hiding her feelings was gone she felt perilously close to tears, but there could be no giving in to them before she got to her room.

Dane came up behind her as she slipped the key in the lock, held the door open, then followed her in, switching on the light in the hall.

'Still sulking?' he asked aloofly.

'I'm not sulking.' In spite of herself her voice had a wobble in it. Terrified that she was going to break down, in the grip of a lassitude so strong that it took all of her strength to keep walking, Meredith moved off towards her room, desperate to reach its sanctuary.

'Meredith!' he said sharply.

'Oh, for heaven's sake!' Tears glinted beneath her lashes, drowning her eyes. 'Haven't you done enough for one night!' she exclaimed, and fled.

Once in her room she tiptoed through to Mark, blessedly sound asleep in his narrow bed beneath the mosquito netting, then locked herself in the bathroom to shower, trying to wash away the whole miserable evening as the warm water pelted her body. After ten minutes or so she wrapped herself in an enormous towel, sat down and removed all her make-up. She was pale, and faint circles beneath her eyes made her look tired, but her mouth was full and red, trembling with suppressed emotion.

At least she had managed to avert tears which would have left her with a hideous headache, but she still felt strung up and nervous, too tense to sleep yet so tired that she couldn't think coherently.

Picking up the hairbrush, she pulled it through her hair, deriving some comfort from the sweeping movements as the bristles parted the heavy tresses. An exploratory hand revealed that the muscles at the back of her neck were so taut they were almost in knots.

Lovely, she thought hollowly, I wonder who caused that? The pirate or his girl-friend; her poisonous innuendoes or his ruthless cruelty?


## CHAPTER SEVEN

THE tap at her door was so soft that she ignored it, thinking it one of the faint night noises. In fact it wasn't until that sixth sense which seemed to operate whenever Dane was near lifted the hairs on the back of her neck that she turned, to see him advancing towards her with a mug in one hand.

'What—what are you doing here?' she whispered, mesmerised by the noiselessness of his approach.

'Bringing you some hot milk.' He set it down on the table beside her bed, and stood looking at her.

Meredith shivered, caught by the unwinking intensity of his gaze as if held motionless in some sudden searchlight.

'Thank you,' she said, fervently wishing that she had put on the gown which hung carelessly across the back of her chair. Although big, the towel revealed too much of her body for her liking. How she wished he would go!

'Make sure you drink it.'

She gave a small, bitter smile. That was more like Dane. 'Yes, of course,' she said, adding, 'my lord.'

'*What* did you say?'

He'd heard, but it seemed that he couldn't believe his ears. And Meredith was already wondering what on earth had impelled her to offer him such provocation.

Stiffly she put the brush down, turning her head so that he could see only the curve of her cheek. 'It doesn't matter. Do you mind going now, Dane? I'm tired, and. . . .'

Her voice trailed away as he moved in the pool of light cast by the lamp; he was still dressed for the ball, still smelt faintly of an old brandy and somebody's fine cigar. Anyone else would have looked incongruous in the feminine room, but as he was Dane, he dominated his surroundings without effort.

'Are you all right?' he asked sharply. 'You're as white as a sheet. Have you had too much to drink?'

Some of her usual fire glimmered for a moment in the depths of her eyes. 'Two glasses of punch? Hardly. Thank you for the milk. I'll drink it, I promise. Now will you go away? I don't need you.'

Ignoring her, as if she was a rebellious child, he moved to stand beside the chair and tipped up her chin, noting the way she winced and turned her head away. Unerringly his hand found the muscles at the back of her neck.

'You're as taut as a violin string,' he said drily as he pulled her to her feet. 'Come on, lie on the bed and I'll give you a neck massage.'

'You?' The idea sent sensuous shivers through her nerves, but she found herself walking obediently towards the bed.

'I have a number of hidden talents,' he confirmed with a hint of mockery underlying the decision in his voice. 'Right, lie down on your stomach.'

Resistlessly she did as she was told, wondering why she was content to be ordered about but unable to summon up the strength to set her will against his.

Dane's hands were wonderfully gentle, kneading the knotted muscles around the base of her neck and across her shoulders with a firm rhythm which brought swift relaxation to her body and brain. Eyelids drooping, she drifted into a sensual lethargy; once she tried to say something, but he hushed her, and soon she was afloat on a sea of lassitude.

Just when his touch began to explore rather than to soothe she never knew, but by the time she became aware of it it was too late. Her weighted eyelids lifted; she felt the smoothness of the sheet against her cheek while his hands moved purposefully down her back to loosen the towel.

'Dane. . . .'

He said nothing. Perhaps he hadn't heard her whispered protest, for when she turned to look into his face there was a dark absorption there which made him incredibly remote. As if drugged she lifted her hand, but his met it and he lifted it to his lips, kissing the palm while his glance rested on her face, devouring the flushed triangle with an emotion she recognised as desire.

Often she had seen films using slow motion for effect. Now, it seemed that time had become stretched, and with it her resistance, to the limit, so that she made no effort to prevent him when he loosened the towel and spread it out to reveal the hidden panorama of her body to his gaze.

'You're beautiful,' he said against her palm, his voice thick yet wondering.

'So are you,' she whispered, and he smiled and pulled her up into his arms, his hands gentle against the satin of her skin.

His mouth moved across her lips. Slowly, as if afraid of frightening her, he traced every curve and plane of her form, touching her with the gentle control of a lover determined to give as well as receive pleasure. Heat gathered in the sensitive areas of her body, giving rise to appetites which could only be slaked by the weight and driving energy of his body.

Meredith ached for him, lifting her arms to slide them around his neck, her head flung back against his arm.

'Are you offering yourself to me?' he muttered against her throat.

'Is that what you want?'

For answer he pulled her close, crushing her breasts against his chest with the fierceness of his passion, his hands rough. 'Yes,' he said harshly. 'But you know that, don't you? You're an expert. How many men have you made love to, Meredith?'

'*Hundreds!*' Without thought her hand came up and she hit him across the cheek, watching with satisfaction as the skin over the bone paled, then reddened. Anger sang swiftly through her veins, anger and frustration and shame for having fallen for his practised seduction. He

had lulled her into lassitude, but he had not really
wanted her; he had shown her with humiliating clearness
just exactly what he thought of her, contemptuously refusing the only thing she could give him, herself.

'Little bitch,' he said, quite gently, holding her still as
she struggled to release herself. 'Was this what you'd
planned for Peter King tonight?'

'No!' she gasped, sickened. 'My God, you've a mind
like a sewer! Why the hell don't you marry Ginny and
then you wouldn't have these frustrations to work off on
whoever happens to get in your way!'

*Danger!* Every instinct warned her, but it took the
black violence of his expression to make her nerves jump
in her body. Apalled at her stupidity, she arched backwards, desperate to free herself before he killed her.

'You might well struggle,' he muttered between his
teeth, his hand relentlessly tangled in her hair. 'It's come
a bit late, though, hasn't it?

When she opened her mouth to scream he covered it
with his, using his weight to tip her off balance into the
pillows. Panic and fear gave her strength, but she was far
too slight to make much impression on him with her fists,
and after that first instinctive attempt to summon help she
remembered Mark, sleeping soundly next door, and knew
she dared not waken him to a scene as sordid as this.

His weight pressed her down on to the sheets and he
smiled as she struggled to push him away, only too
conscious that her movements aroused him sexually.

'Get *off*!' she whispered frantically, pushing at his
shoulders. 'Oh God, I despise you!'

'Not as much as you're going to.'

The threat was viciously delivered; to her horror she
realised that he had every intention of forcing himself on
her with or without her consent. She had wondered what
sort of man lay beneath the hard mask he presented to
the world. Now she was finding out, and the primitive
desire she had unleashed frightened her. And excited her,
for her breath came rapidly through her lips as he
touched her breasts in the most intimate caress she had

ever experienced, his fingers moving across the most sensitive areas with damning skill.

'You're mad,' she groaned, trying to push him away. 'Dane . . . please!'

'Please what? Please make love to me?'

The gibe was earned, for a shattering yearning had sprung to life within her, and when his mouth followed his hands in an exploration of her body she gasped, not in pain but in anticipation of that pain she thought to be inevitable before the promise of an ecstasy only he could give her.

But even as she felt the power of her own passion, realised that she could meet and match his desire, she knew that she could not give in to it. His lovemaking had turned her into a mindless, driven collection of needs and hungers, but she knew with sick certainty that to allow herself the indulgence of accepting him into her body carried a price too high to pay. Pray God she was not too late to stop him.

'*Dane!*' She tightened her fingers on to his hair, jerking his head away from her, meeting the febrile glitter of his gaze with the only thing she could think of that might stop him now. 'Dear God, will you *stop*!' The tears in her eyes spilled over, rendered her voice husky and trembling. 'I—I can't. Not now, not here.'

'The innocent virgin?' he asked thickly, pinioning her hands to her sides with a swift movement which took her completely by surprise. 'Well done, Meredith.'

But she had won, for the terrifying lack of control she had seen in his expression was gone, replaced by the usual mask of self-possession.

And the tears gathered in real earnest. She wept for the sudden coldness of her body, for the fact that he had woken to life a devouring need which she could not allow him to satisfy, for that way lay damnation for her.

'Tears?' There was a surprised note in the deep tones. 'You really are afraid, aren't you?'

'You—you looked as if you wanted to kill me.'

Irony touched his smile, but was qualified by some other emotion—impossible for it to be tenderness, although she suspected it.

Shackled by his cruel grip, she stared mutely at him, her eyes dominating the triangle of her face.

'Don't ever hit me again,' he said softly, releasing her to swing himself upright. Incredibly he was still fully clothed, although the fine material of his shirt was crushed where her fingers had fastened on to it in an effort to bring him even closer.

Her eyes flew from the telltale creases to his profile; more than anything she had ever wanted, she wanted to say something, to touch him so that he would come back and take her completely. Her body ached for him, yearning only for the consummation of her passion, in the sensual oblivion of his arms. But she said nothing, lay as rigid as a statue, putting such a strain on her muscles that she felt paralysed.

'Nothing to say?' He turned and looked down at her, while the hot colour rose to the surface. Smiling narrowly, he pulled the towel so that she was covered. 'You look like a frustrated nymph,' he taunted. 'For your information, Meredith, I don't leave Ginny and come home seething with dark unfulfilled passions, to lie in wait for the first female who crosses my path so that I can have my way with her.'

He was laughing at her, but there was no amusement in his glance.

'You could have fooled me,' she flung, anger making her truculent.

One brow lifted in mocking enquiry. 'Such refreshing modesty! Do you honestly believe I'd behave like that, Meredith?'

'I don't know,' she returned, spacing each word out to gain time for thought.

Once more he was angry, but she no longer feared him. He was fully in command of himself and he wouldn't loose his anger on her again.

Conscious of the penetrating hardness of his gaze, she turned her head, dark lashes fluttering down to cover her eyes. A little sigh escaped through the crushed softness of her mouth.

'I don't know,' she said again. 'Dane, why do you hate me so much? You hated me even before we came, didn't you?'

There was a moment of silence before he answered smoothly, 'Hardly, my dear. I'm not in the habit of disliking on principle.'

'I said *hate*.' She underlined the final word.

He picked up one limp slender hand, turned it over and held it to his mouth. Meredith's eyes flew open in alarm. Beneath her hand he was smiling, that aloof, infuriating smile he used when he was putting her in her place. A shiver of painful pleasure made her skin cold.

'I don't hate you,' he said, his lips brushing her palm. 'I don't know what I feel for you. But I'm going to have to find out, I can see.'

'I think I hate you!'

'Do you?' He chuckled, and put her hand back across her midriff. 'I doubt it, my dear, but think that if it helps your pride.' Incredibly he bent and kissed her eyelids closed again, then touched her mouth with his finger. 'And don't fling any of your favourite adjectives at me. I may be arrogant, conceited, lecherous and thoroughly unbearable, but I know when someone is attracted to me. And lie as much as you want to, my sweet, it's been attraction ever since we set eyes on each other. Now go to sleep.'

Unwillingly, for his closeness set her pulses thundering erratically, Meredith opened her eyes, watching as he walked back across the room.

'Dane.' His name broke from her before she could prevent it.

'The moment's gone,' he said without turning. 'Goodnight, Meredith.'

Minutes after the door had shut firmly behind him she sat up, unwound herself from the towel and flung it on the floor, temper and frustration darkening her eyes. Oh, but she wanted him—and how dangerously close she had been to surrendering everything for a night's pleasure in his arms.

Useless to ask herself why she wasn't the sexually liberated women he thought her. Then she could have taken him to her and not suffered any inevitable aftermath of shame and regret. But that was not her, and as she pulled on her nightgown, looking ruefully at the marks which tomorrow would be faint bruises, she wished vehemently that she had been able to submerge principles and common sense for one night of folly.

When at last she woke the sun was high in the sky, the only noise the liquid trilling of some small bird. Through the window came the sweet perfume of the tiny gardenia flowers, like miniature satin roses. The early morning coolness had gone completely, and although she had only a sheet over her she was unpleasantly hot.

In came Mark, elaborately silent, one brown forefinger held against his mouth.

'Awake!' he called joyously over his shoulder to Renadi, who had remained in his room. He ran across to the bed. 'Time for your b'kf'st.'

'O.K. Kiss me.'

With the spontaneity of childhood he kissed her enthusiastically, cuddling close in her arms.

'Mmm, you smell nice;' she said into the dark silk of his hair. 'What have you been doing?'

'Had mine b'kf'st with Dane, and Nadi and me went for a walk with Suzie.'

Suzie was the enormous Dobermann who guarded the house. She looked as if she would enjoy nothing more than to make a meal of Mark, but had revealed herself to possess a charming temperament. Between her and the small boy had developed one of those friendships which transcended the boundaries of kind. During the day wherever Mark was Suzie was to be found fairly close by.

'And Nadi picked some flowers,' Mark continued. 'Some pick ones and some yellow ones.'

'Pink and yellow,' Meredith corrected, her heart contracting with love. Giving him a tremendous hug, she carried him through to his room where Renadi was replacing the faded hibiscus blooms of yesterday with the ones she had just gathered, threading the flowers on long slivers of cane so that they glowed like enormous silken butterflies against the background of greenery. Even without water the flowers would remain perfect until tomorrow.

Renadi's warm brown glance met Meredith's. 'Have a

nice time last night?' she asked, most of her shyness gone now.

'Lovely,' Meredith lied. 'I didn't get home till after three.'

The wide smile widened, and Renadi chuckled. 'I know. I slept in the room down the hall and I heard you come in.'

For a moment Meredith felt as if she had had the breath knocked out of her. Had she also heard Dane— and if she had, what had she made of the time he had spent in her room? Colour flicked across her cheekbones. What on earth would anyone make of it, except the obvious answer!

Aloud she said casually, 'I'm sorry I woke you. Thank you for keeping an eye on Mark.'

'Oh, I was awake anyway, just about ready to go back to sleep.'

There was no sign of any innuendo in the even sunny tones. She could not have heard Dane. Unless with the Fijian's basic, earthy outlook she considered it quite normal for him to visit Meredith's room for an hour or so at night.

Stooping, Meredith set Mark down. 'Well, if you give me time to have my breakfast first I'll come for a swim with you.'

'We'll meet you down by the pool,' said Renadi.

'Super idea,' Meredith responded. 'I'll get dressed and be out in a minute.'

Swiftly she climbed into shorts and a sun-top, applied a light lipstick and to give her confidence, a touch of her favourite 'Miss Dior' before pulling the sheet back to air the bed.

Aware, as she hung the bath towel on its rack, that her skin was burning once more, she told herself with hard scorn not to be foolish. No one could have made it clearer than Dane that although he found her desirable, to him she was just another in a long procession of nubile women, all of them no doubt considered as sexual partners, many probably discarded because circumstances made it impossible.

In itself passion, even the rushing torrent of hunger which had almost swept them away last night, meant nothing. A matter of chemistry and hormones. What she wanted from Dane was. . . .

Appalled, she collapsed on to the edge of the bed with a thump, her suddenly pinched features revealing her shock. What she wanted from him was his love, in return for hers.

'Fool!' she said aloud, fiercely, eyes dilating enormously above high slanted cheekbones. 'You idiot, you've fallen in love with him.'

And while she tried to convince herself that she could not love a man who despised her so, her hands revealed her secret, twisting together in an agony of supplication.

Mark's voice was a welcome distraction. Swiftly Meredith jumped to her feet, forcing from her features the anguish which had contracted them.

'Come 'n have b'kf'st by the pool,' he called as he ran in the door. 'I can have mine swim then too.'

Meredith looked a question at Renadi.

'Mr Fowler is down there,' the Fijian girl told her. 'He'd like you to go there for your meal.'

Well, the more people around the less time she would have with her thoughts. 'O.K.' She picked up a pair of sunglasses, perching them on her nose. 'Come on, Mark, I'll give you a race!'

There is an art in letting a two-year-old win a race. Meredith possessed it, appearing to run her hardest yet allowing Mark to finish the winner by a very slender margin so that both were flushed and laughing as they came up to the group ensconced under the light shade of the shower tree. Maurice was there, of course, the brightness of the day accentuating the lines of his face, and Dane, and Ginny, coolness personified in a white dress which did wonders for her eyes and hair but inclined her skin to sallowness.

A happy little gathering, Meredith decided bitterly as she scooped Mark up just in time to save him from cannoning into Ginny's long legs.

Oh, how she disliked the creature! The icy forbearance

with which Ginny warded Mark off was bad enough, but the patronising little smile which followed it when the other woman greeted her made Meredith want to tip her into the pool. However, she restrained herself, answering the smooth, barbed remarks about her time of rising with a placid good humour which she had the pleasure of realising annoyed Ginny considerably.

Dane's eyes she would not meet. The memory of last night's interlude and the astounding discovery she had made this morning about her emotions made her so acutely conscious of him that she could hardly bear to look his way. If her life depended on it she could not meet his eyes and see there only cold irony.

So she ate papaya and pineapple with as much relish as she could summon, drank coffee, even took part in the conversation. Mark's presence in the pool, his continual cries of 'Look at me!' made it easier for her to avoid anyone's eye. She turned her chair slightly so that she could pretend to be keeping a close watch on him.

'You do fuss, Meredith,' Ginny observed during a lull. 'Renadi is perfectly trustworthy, I'm sure.'

'I'm sure she is, too.' Meredith drained her coffee, looked blandly across at the older woman. 'But he likes to be watched.'

'Do you think showing off should be encouraged?'

Meredith lifted her brows. 'I don't know that you could call it showing off at his age. But for what it's worth, I think he deserves to be encouraged or he might stop striving.'

'Encouragement, of course, but this dependence is another thing, surely?'

Fortunately at this moment Mark yelled, 'Watch me, Dane! Watch me, Grandy!' and jumped from the edge to land in a shower of spray.

'He's not entirely dependent on me for praise,' Meredith commented drily, watching as he bubbled up to the surface again, his little face split by a broad grin. 'And surely it's rather——' she hesitated substituting for the first word which had sprung to mind, '—rather expecting too much to hope for many signs of independence at his age.'

As if Ginny realised that she had almost been called foolish a patch of red appeared on each cheek. Glancing up at Dane, she asked smilingly, 'And what do you think, my dear? You and Maurice are very silent on the matter.'

Unwillingly Meredith's eyes moved towards him. He appeared tired, yet immensely assured. Looking at Ginny, he replied, 'My knowledge of children is almost non-existent, as I'm sure you're aware, so I'm not equipped to comment. I'd agree that Meredith is inclined to be over-protective, but I think that's understandable. No doubt she'll relax as she gets used to sharing the responsibility.'

Very slightly Meredith's glance widened at this half-compliment. He smiled, shifting his eyes so that they met hers, but there was no expression in the tawny depths at all.

Somehow she had expected to find him different, as though the awakening of her heart and body had evoked some fundamental change in him too. A ridiculous idea, childish and totally unrealistic. He was just the same, dark and dominating, so completely self-sufficient that nothing could penetrate his mask, the firm mouth redeemed from recklessness by self-control. The only consolation she could find was that she knew what he was like when the recklessness overrode the control, and she was almost certain that Ginny Moore, for all that she was the lady in possession, didn't.

'I hope you're right,' Ginny said now, her glance lingering disparagingly on Meredith's face. With a little laugh she added, 'Are you still angry with Dane for preventing you from going to the beach last night? I felt sorry for Peter, but really, both you and he should have known better.'

'What was this?'

Ginny turned to Maurice. 'Haven't they told you yet? A whole crowd of the younger ones decided to go on to a beach and see the dawn in with a bonfire. Fortunately Sarah King told Dane and he insisted on Meredith coming home, so we gave her and Peter a ride back.'

You wouldn't look so happy if you knew what had happened then, Meredith thought maliciously.

Maurice shrugged, those very astute eyes moving from one to another, finally meeting Dane's glance with something like an ironic smile. 'Ah well,' he said tolerantly, 'we're all young once, I suppose.'

If he had expected Dane to justify his action he failed. He merely looked aloof and uncommunicative.

It was Ginny who spoke the words measured as though she suspected that something was happening to which she was not a party. 'It was hardly the thing for Meredith to go to, though, surely? I didn't know half of the young ones who were going and some of them looked as though they'd had too much to drink. Dane was very wise to forbid it, although poor Meredith was furious, of course.'

Meredith's temper threatened to boil once more. Without thought for any consequences she smiled. 'Only for a short time. Dane soon charmed me into a totally different frame of mind.' And she transferred her smile to Dane, allowing it to become very slightly reminiscent.

He lifted one brow at her. 'But you're so easy to charm,' he murmured, cruelly, emphasising all the humiliation she had been trying to forget.

'Oh, do you think so?' she marvelled, pulling her sunglasses back on. 'I thought it was because you're an expert—so experienced at charming birds out of trees.'

Maurice said nothing, his eyes going from one to the other while a peculiarly grim smile touched his mouth. But Ginny looked angry, and then hid it with an effort.

'Do I detect a certain amount of tension?' she asked archly, touching Dane's arm with possessive fingers. 'I suppose you had another battle after you got home?'

'You could call it that,' Dane agreed maddeningly, every word carefully chosen to hurt as his glance flickered rapierlike over Meredith's countenance. 'Meredith rides her passions hard, and God help those who get in her way.'

Although Ginny appeared to accept his words at face value there was a glitter of suspicion in her gaze. 'It's incredible, isn't it? With colouring like that she should be cool and demure, instead of possessing a temper like the reddest of red heads. You really must learn to control yourself, Meredith; I'm sure both Dane and Maurice will agree with me when I say that nothing is so offputting as a bad-tempered woman. Aren't I right, Maurice?'

The pretty little air of deference with which she appealed to him released the stringent stopper Meredith had put on her temper. Standing up, she put her glasses on the table, yawned and said, 'I'm sure you are, Ginny, as always. Now, if you'll excuse me, I promised Mark a swim.'

And she dived straight into the water, careless of what construction any of them put on her discourtesy. Damn them both, she fumed, striking out for the other side of the pool, Damn Ginny for being so patronisingly bitchy, and double damn Dane for driving a spear straight into her heart. Cruel devil, with his caustic tongue and cold eyes!

Without paying them any attention she played with Mark, trying to ease the pain in his uncomplicated company. But after a while her conscience began to nag; she had been unpardonably rude, and she owed Maurice, if nobody else, good manners. So she hauled herself up on to the side of the pool, pushed her hair from her face and sat quietly, waiting for Maurice to finish speaking. Her blouse and shorts clung wetly to her, making her regret that she had made such a stupid gesture as going in with her clothes on.

'Cooled off?' Maurice sounded amused rather than censorious.

'Yes.' She lifted her eyes and said quietly, 'Thoroughly, thank you. Ginny's quite right, my temper is appalling.' A glint of mischief would not be banished as she continued, 'I suppose I'll just have to reconcile myself to becoming a sour old maid.'

'Hardly an apology.' Dane's voice was implacable.

Refusing to look at him, Meredith said directly to Ginny, 'I'm sorry if I made you angry.'

'Not at all, but you must see for yourself that my comment was justified.' The other woman was pleased, unable to resist the temptation to add, 'That blouse is indecent. You'd better get changed.'

The wet blouse clung and Meredith had worn no bra

beneath it. She could see the dusky shape of her nipples through the thin cotton. A slow flush heated the skin on her neck as she stood up.

'O.K.,' she said, glad to be leaving. 'Come on, Mark, time to go, angel.'

'I'll come with you,' Maurice told her. Dane helped him to his feet and the old man stood for a moment to regain his breath. With Mark loudly protesting but amenable by her side Meredith watched her grandfather, frowning. Was it just her imagination or had he weakened considerably even since she had come to Fiji? She knew better than to comment on it, but slipped her arm beneath his as they began the walk back to the house.

'Don't you trust me to get there under my own steam?' he demanded.

'I've no doubt that you would, even if you had to crawl.'

He grinned. 'Well, I may have slowed down, but my brain is still as good as ever it was, even if Ginny Moore has decided I'm in my dotage. And don't you forget it!'

He seemed not at all put out by the assessment of Ginny's attitude, but the acid comment made Meredith wonder if perhaps he was changing his mind about the woman's suitability for Dane.

'I think you're a bit harsh,' she said, trying to be objective.

He slanted her a swift, sharp sideways glance. 'You're a liar. You can't bear the woman. What will you do when she marries Dane?'

Hoping that her expression didn't reveal the swift anguish his question caused, she hesitated, then shrugged. 'I don't know. Will they—will they live here?'

'Yes.'

'Then I suppose I'll have to go somewhere else.' With a throat dry as sand she added, 'I doubt very much if we could share a house.'

'We'll see.' They walked for a few steps further before he said abruptly, 'I'm going to summon a meeting of the executives of the firm. There'll be—oh, sixteen men, and usually ten wives come too. Think you can handle it?'

'Yes,' she said simply.

'Good. I'll discuss it with Dane and let you know when they're coming, but probably in a week's time.'

## CHAPTER EIGHT

IT was strange to meet so many relatives she had never heard of, to know that many of these smooth, sophisticated men and women had known her mother. Meredith found herself looking at them with a faint query, wondering if any would talk to her about Dinah.

Somehow her mother had receded into the past; it was difficult for Meredith to reconcile the quiet contented woman she had known with the young girl who had hated her father and run away with a man she scarcely knew just to get away from her home. Why, she didn't even know how Dinah felt about her unsatisfactory husband.

An odd pair of parents, she thought wryly, smiling at a couple introduced as Mr and Mrs Philip Lamont. They were the last of the guests, but certainly not the least important. And with them they had someone whom Meredith had last seen on Hibiscus Island.

'Don!' she exclaimed, smiling with genuine pleasure as she held out her hand in greeting.

'Hey—Meredith!' He looked as astonished as she felt, taking her hand as if she were a very rare and precious gem. 'Where on earth did you spring from?'

'I live here,' she told him.

Maurice interposed, the hard old voice aloof. 'Meredith is my granddaughter, Mr Poole. I believe you and your family were kind to her when she and Mark stayed on Hibiscus Island.'

Meredith could have wept at the rapid change in Don's attitude. His friendly camaraderie turned to awe as he answered diffidently, 'It was no trouble, sir. My mother took a real fancy to Meredith and the little boy.'

'No doubt,' Maurice said smoothly. 'It was kind of you, nevertheless. Meredith had recently lost her parents and was unaware of what life here was going to be like. I have my granddaughter's assurance that the week she spent in your family's company gave her the rest she needed so badly. Why don't you show Mr Poole round the garden, Meredith? I'm sure Philip doesn't need him for half an hour or so.'

Oh, he did it superbly, effectively stressing that whatever their relationship before, an enormous gulf existed between them now. Seething, yet impotent, Meredith listened to Philip Lamont's disclaimers, gave her grandfather one scorching look which affected him not at all and led Don off.

At first she filled in the awkward minutes by asking after his family. When that palled they were by her lookout and she showed him the faint purple dot on the sea which was Hibiscus Island.

'When we were there, did you know Mr Fowler was your grandfather?' he asked abruptly.

'Yes.'

He brooded for a moment. 'Then I suppose I have you to thank for this job.'

Meredith lifted her brows. 'Why on earth—I didn't mention you at all!'

'Just a holiday romance?' He smiled wryly into her worried face. 'Only a couple of kisses hardly constitute a romance.'

'Hardly,' she said, wondering just what he meant by his cryptic comments about the job. 'Don——'

From behind them Dane's voice was faintly frosty.

'I'm afraid Mark has hurt himself, Meredith, and is crying for you.'

As she swung around Meredith caught a gleam of some undetermined emotion in his eyes. Within a second it had faded to his usual cold smoothness. His hearing was acute, so he must have heard that revealing exchange with Don. Almost she was pleased, but it made her position here more perilous. If once Dane began to wonder about that promiscuity he held against her it would be only a short step to making enquiries.

Not very much to her surprise it appeared that he and Don knew each other, even if only by sight. She didn't really need to be told that for some strange reason the Fowlers had lured Don into their net, presumably to keep an eye on him. But why? It galled to see the awed respect with which he responded to Dane.

Mark had been comforted into smiles when they arrived back at the house. Unable to rid herself of the suspicion that he had merely been an excuse for Dane to follow them, Meredith was extremely cool to her cousin for the rest of the day while playing her part as hostess with a skill which pleased Maurice. Ironically it seemed that she had become necessary to him.

And without her surrendering any of her independence. Maurice liked her to look attractive, to charm his older friends and dazzle the younger ones, at the same time preserving an aloofness which it pleased him to think of as the Fowler touch. In return he gave her a home and an allowance, and the independence she wanted. There could never be love between them, but at least they respected each other.

But Dane . . . No, now was not the time to think of Dane, who smirched her with his every look, who taunted her with wantonness and despised her for succumbing to his practised technique. She hated Dane. Yes, and loved him too.

The rest of the day passed uneventfully, with Don firmly in his place as an employee of the vast Fowler empire, graciously permitted to mix with the supermen at the top. He would do very well, she thought critically. Already the somewhat casual manners had been honed and refined into something approaching urbanity. Before long he would have acquired a degree of sophistication which would enable him to hold his own in the world he aspired to. Perhaps he was lucky that he had kissed her on a starry tropical night with Dane only a few yards away.

Dinner was a success. The menu, so carefully planned with Joe, met with everyone's approval; they told her so, these elegant women and their watchful husbands. Tomorrow they were all going out to one of the outer islands where Maurice had a beach house. There they would swim and laze the day away while the men did a spot of fishing. So far there had not been a word of business spoken. No doubt the conference would be held the day after that when the wives were to be despatched to do some duty-free shopping at Lautoka, followed by a fashion show to be held in the air-conditioned comfort of one of the big hotels at Nadi.

Great was the name of Fowler, Meredith had thought drily when she rang for tickets some days ago. There had been no trouble at all in acquiring them. Indeed, the girl had been obsequiously eager in her response.

Following that there would be a cocktail party to which Maurice's friends had been invited as well as the local leaders of all races. And after that, thank heavens, the whole lot would take off, the top men and their wives in the private jet, the subordinates relegated to the commercial airline.

Meredith would be glad to see them go. She had had enough of their well-disguised curiosity, the delicate probings to see if she knew exactly where Maurice had slotted her and Mark into his will, the keenness with which they observed her every movement. Besides, with them gone Ginny Moore and her mother would not need to haunt the house.

The sooner Dane announced his engagement to Ginny the better, she told herself with a hard practicality which almost hid the pain in her heart. Once the marriage was fait accompli she might be able to root out this forbidden love from her life and get on with making some sort of existence for herself. An existence without Dane might seem horribly dreary, but she had no doubt that she could cope with it. Life did not end because one loved unwisely, and after a while there would be happiness again, perhaps even love.

Unfortunately, while her head told her all of this her heart rejected it, and whenever she felt his eyes on her she could not prevent the blood from coursing through her veins with all of the reckless passion of youth.

It humiliated, this effortless physical power he wielded

over her. Every time her pulses raced to his casual touch or the sound of his voice she had to will herself not to betray the effect he had on her. It made her very cool towards him, meeting the gold of his eyes with the faintest challenge in the limpid depths of hers, her smile withdrawn, reserved, her manners impeccable.

'A true Fowler,' so Mrs Philip Lamont told her as they lay in the shade of the coconut palms which bent their feathery plumes above the beach house.

It was meant as a compliment. Meredith smiled as if she accepted it as one, her eyes hidden behind glasses so that their expression could not be read. It was very hot, very still on the island. Tiny lizards darted and hid on the hot sands and among the litter of leaves and driftwood; far out to sea a faint white dot showed where Dane's yacht headed towards them. It had been out all day with the men. Ostensibly they were fishing, but Meredith had no doubt that today had seen conducted the preliminaries of tomorrow's meeting. A certain amount of testing and probing, probably a time to weigh up opposition and muster support.

At least they all knew each other well, she thought thankfully, these guests who were all so much older than her. Certain tensions had made themselves apparent, but as their husbands were colleagues so the wives necessarily ran in harness too, although it seemed that some felt less than liking for each other. However, none was prepared to blot any copybook under Maurice's eyes. So they smiled and gossiped and dozed and sipped fruit juice, but because they were all at the age when figures needed watching, ate next to none of the snacks which Joe had prepared.

No doubt the men would demolish those. On the flat ground behind the beach an earth oven was slowly steaming; for those who disliked the distinctive smoky taste of the *lovo*, a sucking pig roasted on a spit, basted with a spicy sauce by Joe.

After dinner there would be a *meke*, and the evening would end with a slow cruise home beneath the stars. Meredith, with Joe's help, had gone over the arrange-

ments several times and could think of nothing she had
missed, but she could not help anxiously wondering if she
had forgotten something so vital and obvious that everyone would spot it. She had no doubt they would be kind,
but it would be humiliating to have her shortcomings
shown up before guests. And Maurice would be disap-
pointed, she thought, carefully avoiding the thought of the
only Fowler she wished to impress.

'Are you missing your brother?' Mrs Lamont enquired
soothingly. 'You mustn't become over-protective, my
dear. He'll be quite safe without you.'

'Oh, I'm not worrying in the least about Mark,' Meredith returned, not entirely truthfully. 'Renadi is very reli-
able and he's not given to mischief.'

'A dear little boy,' her companion said vaguely, adding
what was evidently her highest accolade. 'A true Fowler.'

Again Meredith smiled, subduing the temptation to
yell out that their names were Colfax and surely there
must be something of their father in them!

Against the smoky haze of one of the outer islands the
yacht tacked towards them, the sails filling as a puff of
wind caught them. Meredith sat up, her hands clasping
her ankles as the slender beautiful thing came creaming
through the gap in the reef, one of the Fijian deckhands
keeping lookout in the bow. On, on it came, close enough
for her to see that Dane was at the helm; then there was a
sharp explosion of orders and the yacht came broadside
to the shore, sails fell and with a rattle two anchors went
down.

A few minutes later the men were ashore, expansive,
slightly burned by the wind and the sea, bearing with
them fish which they insisted be prepared for dinner.

Followed an hour during which everyone freshened up
before drifting out on to the wide terrace to indulge in
drinks before dinner. It should have been a pleasant time,
this period when the cooler air drove away the lassitude
of the day, and everyone relaxed into camaraderie.

Perhaps it was. Certainly there was a lot of laughter
and chaffing, even some very mild flirtation, but Meredith was left with the taste of ashes in her mouth for

Ginny and Dane seemed inseparable. The sight of them together made her desperate with an emotion she recognised as anguish.

'You're quiet.' Maurice's shrewd eyes scanned the contours of the face.

'Don't tell anyone,' she hissed, 'but I'm terrified something is going to go wrong.'

He looked astonished. 'What on earth could go wrong?'

'It's easy enough for you ' she began heatedly, only to have him interrupt.

'Dane, come and take this girl away somewhere to cool her off,' he ordered blandly, adding, 'Ginny, pander to an old man's whim and talk to me. I need someone restful. Meredith is like a cat on hot bricks.'

Fuming, Meredith resigned her place to the older woman, who appeared torn between jealousy and a smug intolerance. But as Dane escorted her across the floor to where Vasilau dispensed drinks she felt Ginny's eyes boring into her back.

'Relax,' said Dane after a moment. 'You have a talent for organisation, as I'm sure you know. Nothing's going to come unstuck.'

'Don't you believe it!' She was gloomy, hiding with words the singing delight his nearness brought to her.

He laughed, and took a glass of sherry from a tray. 'Here, soothe your nerves with that.'

The only nerves which needed calming were those stretched by his presence, but she accepted the drink, turning her head to hide the flush which his fingers on hers brought to her cheeks.

'I didn't intend you to drain it at one gulp,' he commented mildly after a moment, his mouth lifting in the one-cornered smile she found so endearing.

Meredith gazed at the half empty glass with dismay. 'I forgot it wasn't fruit juice,' she apologised. 'I suppose it was some rare vintage.'

'Sherry is a blend, my child, not a vintage.'

Incredibly it seemed that for tonight at least he was to forget his dislike and distrust. As they walked slowly across the wide terrace he told her of the enormous bodegas at Jerez in Spain where sherry had its birthplace, and from there took her on a swift tour of Europe.

He had the gift of describing a scene or incident in a few spare phrases which brought them vividly to life, and as his knowledge of Europe was wide she listened, fascinated, occasionally asking a question or making a comment.

'Never been there?'

He sounded surprised. Meredith shook her head. 'No. There wasn't enough money.' On an impulse she asked, 'Dane, did you ever meet my mother?'

'Yes,' he answered calmly, moving with her to a small arbour where corralita hung in heart-shaped panicles of bloom.

'Did you like her?'

'Yes, I did. Why, Meredith?'

'I don't know,' she said on a sigh. 'I've realised that she was an intensely private person, and that I didn't really know her. I don't like to ask Maurice about her, but there's no one else I trust.'

'Do you trust me?'

The setting sun dazzled her, so that when she looked at him all she could see was his outline, but there had been an odd note in his voice which made her cautious.

'Of course,' she returned abruptly.

After a moment he said, 'Dinah was a pretty girl, not beautiful as you are, but with charm but not much depth of character. I was ten when I saw her last and self-centred like all kids of that age, but I knew even then that she was afraid of Maurice.'

'I think she was afraid of him the day she died,' she said.

'Are you afraid of him?'

Eyes wide, she shook her head.

'No,' he said, with something like satisfaction. 'That's why he likes you. He despised your mother.'

'And she hated him, but let him support us all until she died.'

Against the vivid evening sky his shoulders moved in a shrug. 'Don't judge her too harshly, Meredith.'

'I don't judge her at all.' But I wish I'd known, she thought miserably. If she had known that Maurice was not the ogre Dinah had thought him then perhaps she might not have started this masquerade. And perhaps when Dane looked at her he might not see a precocious brat with an illegitimate child. No, he'd see a precocious brat who had gone to bed with Don Poole, she thought, lashing herself with the knowledge of his contempt. Or, at the very last, been indiscreet. And her subsequent response to his lovemaking could only reinforce his suspicions.

'What did she tell you of the set-up here?' asked Dane.

'Nothing.' After a moment she said, 'She told me about Maurice, of course; she warned me that he was autocratic.'

'I suspect you're softening her view of him.' Dane's voice was grim, but there was no anger in it.

'As you said, she was afraid of him. And afraid for Mark. I think she knew I could stand up for myself, but Mark——' Her voice faded as she realised how close she had come to giving the show away.

'But Mark——' he prompted.

Before she continued she moved so that the sun no longer hid his expression, her eyes searching his face. She learned nothing from the mask he presented to her. Even the yellow fires within his eyes were banked.

'Well, he's only a baby. And you must admit Maurice spoke like a tyrant the first time we met.'

'Testing you,' Dane told her almost indifferently.

'Oh.' She was silent, thinking this over, her brow furrowed as she looked down into the tawny sherry.

'You passed.'

She looked up, her expression set. 'And the way you spoke—was that a test, too?'

With no attempt to evade the issue he said quietly, 'No, I meant it.'

'And would say the same again, I suppose,' she said bitterly, realising only then how much he could hurt her.

His eyes held hers, topaz-hard, implacable. 'In the same circumstances, yes.' As she turned, impelled by the pain within her to get as far away from him as possible, he put his hand on her shoulder.

Like a rabbit held in thrall by a snake, she froze, only the dilation of her pupils revealing that the sensuous smoothing of her skin was arousing sensations she had thought never to feel again.

'But I've learned a lot about you since then,' he said blandly.

A voice called his name; without removing his hand he walked her out of the arbour and took her with him into a group, caring nothing for the knowledgeable eyes which watched them.

The evening assumed a dreamlike quality for Meredith. It could have been the tropical splendour of the night, or the ambience created by good food and wine and people determined to enjoy themselves, but everything ran as smoothly as silk. Beautiful people having a wonderful time, she thought as she watched the magnificent *masi*-clad Fijians dancing in the light of flaring torches, their dark faces intent as they interpreted each song, sometimes warlike, sometimes tender, frequently sparkling with humour.

Afterwards there was much more sedate dancing on the terrace, during which Meredith had ample time to watch Dane effortlessly charming every other woman there. Incredible, she thought numbly, worn out with being polite and charming herself. Absolutely incredible how in this group of masterful men he drew the eyes, he and Maurice both. But Dane possessed a sexual charisma which made women eye him speculatively, even those who were happily married. And there was envy in their husbands' glances, as well as respect.

Useless to tell herself that she would get over him. Men like Dane, with that rare combination of flint-hard integrity and passion, were few on the ground and the women who loved them legion. Thanks to Ginny Meredith knew that he found his adorers boring; it buoyed up her resolution not to let this new attitude of his con her into dropping her guard.

She came perilously close to it, however, when they

danced together. It took all of her will power and her best social manner to hide the riding tide of desire which he invoked with his nearness.

After a few minutes he looked down at her, a gleam of appreciation lighting up his smile. 'Meredith, shut up,' he said softly, pulling her closer to him.

If she opened her mouth now it would be to address his shoulder. Suddenly it seemed an excellent idea to rest her head there, but after the lightest pressure she pulled back, appalled by the fever in her blood.

'Tired?' he enquired smoothly, so close to her ear that his breath warmed the lobe, sending an exquisite thrill through her nerves.

'Yes.' It was a lie.

'You're doing well, sweet cousin. But I'm sure you're aware of it.'

The old taunting note was back in his voice. It hit like a blow, but gave her the necessary strength to say with her usual asperity, 'No doubt it comes from the Fowler side of me.'

Dane laughed, sliding his arms across her back to prevent her from pulling away. 'No doubt, my dear. Poor Dinah really gave you a complex about us, didn't she?'

Stonily she gazed over his shoulder to where Ginny danced with one of the unattached executives. They appeared to be getting on like a house on fire. It helped to remember that she was looking at the woman Dane planned to marry, otherwise she might have surrendered to the yearning need she felt and done something foolish. Like relax in his arms and rest her cheek against him, abandon herself to the wildness which was clamouring for expression within her.

'I suppose she did,' she said. 'I'd rather not talk about it.'

'You asked me about her before.'

Stung, she lifted her eyes, met the sardonic amusement of his. 'You—you were approachable then, not—not sarcastic and superior.'

Something flickered in the depths of his glance, then the hard mouth relaxed into a smile, mocking yet not unkind. 'Dear me, what an unpleasant character you make me out to be!'

'You can hardly expect me to like you,' she pointed out, dragging her eyes away from his face in self-defence.

'I suppose not. But you aren't indifferent to me, are you?'

'What do you mean?' she faltered, paling beneath her tan.

'Don't pretend to be stupid. I know just how your heart beats beneath my mouth.'

A flush swept over her skin, caused not by shame, but by the erotic imagery his words had given rise to.

'That's a purely physical reaction—in that way, no, I'm not indifferent to you.'

'Relax,' he drawled, contempt chilling his tones. 'You know for a woman of experience you're remarkably bashful. You react like the greenest adolescent.'

'I think—I think you're trying to upset me,' she said faintly, bending her head so that he could not see how his words affected her.

'And succeeding, if that very becoming blush is any indication,' he murmured, dropping his voice so that no one else, however close, could hear. 'Does the idea of having me for a lover frighten you so much? You respond very nicely when I make love to you. I'm sure that as you're a woman of such experience you could accommodate yourself to me very easily.'

'Will you *stop* it!' she hissed, driven almost mad by the openly sensual note in his voice. 'I wouldn't—I can't——' Desperately she flung at him, 'You're going to marry Ginny Moore.'

'It doesn't look like it, does it?' As he spoke he indicated Ginny and her partner, dancing together in an embrace which could only be termed clinging.

Bewildered, Meredith met his eyes, saw there nothing but mockery. 'But she said——'

'Did she?' He looked suddenly, savagely angry so that she pulled away, only to be hauled back against him hard, as if his patience had snapped. 'She had no right to surmise so much.'

'But Grandfather told me that you and she were almost engaged.'

'Really?' An arrogantly lifted brow disposed of Maurice. 'He's felt for some time that it's time I was married. Ginny was one of several contenders.'

This cold-blooded dismissal made Meredith furiously angry. Without thinking she blurted, 'Well, you needn't think you can add me to the list. I'm not available, now or ever!'

'Never is a long time,' he responded coolly, then the music stopped, and Meredith was so thankful that she allowed him to keep his arm around her waist as they walked to where Maurice sat.

'You look hot,' her grandfather observed, eyeing her flushed cheeks and sparkling eyes with grim amusement.

'No. I've just been quarrelling with Dane,' she retorted sweetly.

She did not miss the swift searching glance which Maurice sent above her head, nor the way his mouth relaxed into a smile, and the suspicion which had been born in the minutes of the dance hardened into near-certainty. They were up to something, and although she fought against the knowledge she was almost certain she knew what it was.

Looking from one to the other she saw satisfaction in her grandfather's expression, a formidable reserve in Dane's. This time the contempt was in her glance.

'If you'll excuse me,' she said quietly, and made her way slowly through the clan, who suddenly became expansive. Gone was the watchfulness behind which they had sheltered. They had been waiting to see which way the wind blew, and now they thought they knew. *Never!* Meredith thought fiercely, unaware that her resolution gave her a haughty beauty which linked her to the arrogant strength in both Dane and her grandfather's features.

'Anything wrong?' Philip Lamont's wife asked in the cloakroom.

Meredith started, then relaxed, the angry glitter dying from her eyes. 'No,' she said, adding with a wry smile, 'I could beat Dane and Maurice over the heads with a chair, but apart from that everything is fine.' She liked Mrs Philip and had an instinctive knowledge that in spite of her vagueness she was to be trusted. At the moment she yearned for her mother; something about the older woman reminded her of Dinah.

'Well, it happens,' Mary agreed now, smiling into the mirror above the vanity. 'Even the best of men can be very exasperating.'

'And no one could call either of those two terrors the best of men,' Meredith said jerkily, running cold water over her wrists in an effort to cool down.

'My dear, you cope very well with them. It's easy to see that Maurice is proud of you and——' Mary paused, then shrugged. 'Why pick my words with such care? I'm sure you prefer plain speaking. Dane is never obvious, but I've no doubt he respects you. And that's important, you know.'

If only she knew! But Meredith couldn't confide in her however much she wanted to. Aloud she said, 'When he isn't playing lord of all creation, no doubt.'

'He's so *masterful*,' Mrs Philip sighed, lavishly spraying herself with perfume. 'It's a Fowler trait, and there's no fighting it. I suppose that's why you resent it; you do have your fair share, don't you?'

In the mirror Meredith met limpid brown eyes with something like shock. 'Masterful?' she stammered. '*Me?*'

'Yes, you.' The older woman was serene. 'How many nineteen-year-olds would be able to cope with a gathering like this?'

'But—I've been terrified . . .' Meredith's voice trailed away. 'I have, you know . . .'

'You see? You may have found it a strain, but you've coped, haven't you? Oh, you'll make a wonderful wife for—for any man.'

And bestowing a sweet smile on her, Mary left, trailing perfume like a particularly well-endowed rose bush.

For 'any man' read 'Dane', Meredith said shakily to herself as she re-applied lipstick. A fierce yearning clutched her, weakening her so that she gripped the marble vanity, staring down as her fingers whitened. Oh, to be Dane's wife, to know the ecstasy of surrendering to his desire! Her eyes darkened, the pupils widening as the fierce, sensuous images wreaked havoc on her body. Very deliberately she pressed a wet cottonwool ball to her face. No doubt it was an immensely satisfactory solution; she would be cared for, Mark would make a father of the man he already adored, and Dane would have a complaisant, efficient wife. A neat tidying up of all loose ends. Maurice could die happy in the knowledge that his empire was safe.

'Like hell!' she told her reflection stormily.

The moon was low when they set off for Lautoka, a silver crescent worn over black velvet, set amidst diamonds. Such a slender, graceful new moon, adding glamour to the night yet providing so little light that the deck was in pleasant darkness.

Apart from a few of the hardened drinkers most of the clan sat about on deck, talking in soft voices until one of the younger members produced a guitar and began to tune it. Urged on, he began to sing and soon was joined by almost everyone, including the crew. From the galley came trays of small savouries and clear jellied soup, ideal for clearing the head.

They sang folk songs and pops, finishing up with that best known of all Australian songs *Waltzing Matilda* as they came up to the wharf.

But the most beautiful song of all, the one that brought tears to Meredith's eyes, was the crew's rendition of *Isa Lei* the men's deep voices providing a gonglike accompaniment to the high, pure tones of the women. It was Fiji's best-loved song and she had heard it dozens of times, but the pathos always left her shaken. And to her delight she discovered that she was beginning to understand the words, so the hours spent speaking stumbling Fijian to Renadi and Litia's giggles had not been wasted.

When at last all was quiet, every guest bedroom silent, she spared a glance at her watch, astounded to discover that it was only one o'clock. Six hours' sleep, and then another exhausting day, for tomorrow night was the big party.

At least there was no time to think of the suspicions she had formed during this evening. She was so exhausted that she couldn't remember getting into bed.

Those suspicions were brought back to her early enough the next morning. With Renadi and a bright, noisy Mark she crept down to the pool, hoping that a swim would put paid to the thickness in her head. And there was Dane, doing the fiftieth of his daily hundred laps. He lifted a hand in careless greeting but continued on his way, purposeful as ever.

For a moment Meredith fought the cowardly desire to turn tail, before dropping her wrap and diving in. When she broke the surface Mark was yelling, 'Me too, me too, Meddy!' as he prepared to jump into her arms.

They played for some minutes before she relinquished him to Renadi and struck out on her own, keeping to the opposite side of the pool from Dane.

This was the pattern of the days that followed. Without being obvious she tried to make sure that they were never alone, using her position as hostess as a barrier between them. That Dane knew what she was doing was obvious right from the start, but apparently he agreed with her decision, no doubt using the time to disengage himself gracefully from Ginny, Meredith thought spitefully. That lady seemed to have found solace with one of the younger executives. Meredith had no doubt that the Fowler Mafia had somehow manipulated things that way; Ginny was no longer needed, so she was dumped in the most civilised way. Presumably pressure of the same insidious sort would be brought to bear on her if she proved recalcitrant.

Well, she was not Ginny Moore, and if Maurice and Dane had decided between them that she was to marry Dane they would find that she was every bit as stubborn as the worst Fowler. They could not force her to the altar, she thought somewhat hysterically, hiding her awareness that they had an excellent lever in Mark. And in her reluctant love for Dane. Only they did not know of that. Dane knew that he excited her, that he could make her want him, but her love was a secret he must never know. Because if he did, he wouldn't hesitate to use it, she knew.

How could she love a man as ruthless as a sophisticated Attila the Hun? Because, her instinct told her, she needed someone with strength to match her own.

She was thankful when the last of the entourage left Nadi airport, taking Ginny and her mother with them. The strain of coping with them had been considerable, but she was also regretful. No doubt the softening up process would now begin.

Instead life went on as before. Dane worked. Flew to Suva and Australia and the Philippines, was mocking but distant when he was home and spent long hours in his office.

Maurice increased her allowance, ignoring her protests, and spent a considerable amount of *his* time pursuing his acquaintance with Mark. Slowly, imperceptibly, she began to relax, deciding that perhaps she had merely been indulging in wishful thinking. The days lengthened, became hotter as the dry season progressed towards summer: the doves cooed languorously in the raintrees night and morning.

Then Ginny came back, arriving unheralded one day, slender and svelte, her dark hair cut and set by a master in the lastest fashion.

'I had it done in Sydney,' she said when Meredith complimented her on it. 'Sean's mother always goes to him.'

'Sean?'

'Sean McDermott.' The cool eyes flickered over Meredith's face. 'He was here with the family.'

'Oh—yes.' Feeling that she had been gauche, Meredith said, 'I'm afraid Dane is still in Manila, and Maurice has taken a trip to one of the farms in the Highlands.'

'I came to see you,' Ginny told her. 'I see you aren't wearing a ring yet.'

Meredith's eyes widened. 'I beg your pardon?'

'Oh, don't play the innocent with me! You know

damned well what I'm talking about. Dane's ring— in Sydney they're all waiting breathlessly for the announcement.'

As if she had been hit Meredith's head jerked, then was still. 'Then they'll wait a long time,' she said as calmly as she could.

'Don't tell me you didn't know?' Ginny leaned forward, her glance hard and malicious, a tight smile distorting her patrician features. 'How stupid you must be! Surely you know what sort of people you're dealing with by now, or do you still think of them as cousin Dane and your kindly old grandfather?'

The savage sarcasm in her tones made Meredith pale, but she controlled her instinctive repulsion. 'I'd rather you didn't——'

'What you'd rather is neither here nor there! For just this once you're going to listen to me, you smug little interloper, and I don't care how you feel about it. Your charming grandfather has decided—and I have this on the best of authority, Dane's—that you'll make your cousin an excellent wife. And because Dane is every bit as ruthless and autocratic as Maurice he's going to put aside the fact that you've borne a child——' she laughed at the white shock her words caused. 'Oh yes, Dane told me about that little embarrassment when I was still the main contender in the field.'

Through lips that were stiff with pain Meredith said, 'Will you *stop* this? For heaven's sake——'

'No, for *my* sake, and you're going to listen to every last word I've got to say. Whenever Dane makes love to you you'll know damned well that he's despising you for sleeping around, as well as wishing that you were me. Oh, you've got every trick well learned; you look like a high-class slut, with promises in every glance, every movement you make, but Dane loves *me*. He always will, because I refused to leap into bed with him like every other woman he's ever wanted.'

Every word stung, poison-tipped, painful because Meredith knew that they were true.

Drawing a breath which hurt, she said with painful

concentration, 'I think this conversation is too degrading. Please——'

'Degrading!' The older woman laughed shrilly. 'How can anything degrade you further? How many men have you had, beside Mark's father and Dane?'

'Dane?' Meredith's head whipped around. Ginny was smiling, a dreadful hungry smile which made her shiveringly evil.

Now she answered softly, 'Yes, *Dane*. How stupid you are! Don't you know that servants are the biggest gossips in the world? He's been seen, you fool, and he knows it. All the Fijians are waiting for you to marry. Why else do you think he's decided to marry you? He's tough enough to withstand pressure from Maurice, but his own honour is more important to him than love. What was he like?' She leaned forward, her blue eyes avid and eager. 'Exciting? How did you feel when he——'

'Ginny, this is intolerable! Stop it! I have no intention of marrying Dane!' Meredith felt nausea rising swiftly through her body. 'You're not well,' she said after a moment, afraid of the febrile intensity of the other woman's gaze, the tic that twitched in the skin above her jawline.

'Sick for love,' said Ginny, struggling visibly for self-control. After a ghastly moment she attained it; the glitter died from her eyes. Strangely remote, she said, 'You've got no hope, you know. I almost feel sorry for you. I can't think of anything worse than to be married to Dane knowing that he feels nothing but contempt and lust for you. You'll live in a hell of humiliation and pain, and all so no one else gets their hands on the shares Maurice will leave you!'

'Maurice will make sure that things are tied up,' Meredith returned crisply, using one of the arguments with which she had tried to convince herself. 'There's no need for Dane to make a sacrifice of himself.'

Her companion leaned forward, fully in control of herself once more, aiming each word like a dart, to sting and poison wherever they touched. 'I can see you don't want to believe me, but you'll see, in time. Oh, we're all very civilised; they've found Sean for me, and I'll marry him, because that way you and I will meet quite often and I'll be able to watch you disintegrate.'

The gloating pleasure with which she enunciated the words horrified and frightened Meredith. 'I think you'd better go home,' she said, made gentle by her compassion for the other woman's misery. 'I'll get Joe to drive you.'

'Wait!' As Meredith rose to her feet Ginny got there too, her hand fastening around Meredith's wrist with paralysing strength. 'You don't really believe me, do you. Well, you will. Oh, you think you're strong enough to cope with anything, but Dane is a Devil. He'll use the fact that you love him——' She stopped and laughed as Meredith whitened. 'He knows, you little fool. Of course he knows. He told me—he was quite amused—before Maurice got this—this maggot in his brain. And he'll use it, force you to marry him, then you'll learn what hell is like, Meredith.'

With a gesture as vicious as it was unexpected she lifted her hand and scratched, with one long, immaculate fingernail, a groove into the tender skin below Meredith's ear. 'Just to remember me by,' she purred, and with a return to her normal gracious air of patronage swept through the door into the hall. Trembling, Meredith waited until the sound of the car died away. Then she ran, as if hell was at her heels, to the courtyard where Mark was playing with his toys. To his surprise she snatched him up and held him tightly, her face buried in the sweet-smelling cap of dark curls while her heart raced, then slowly—oh, how slowly—settled back to its normal rhythm.

'C'y?' Mark enquired anxiously, pushing up her head to peer into her eyes.

'No, I'm not crying,' she told him, but her attempt at laughter came perilously close to a sob.

'Play Mark.'

She had to force herself to listen to his prattle, but at least while she was with him the spectre of Ginny's distorted features as she mouthed poison stayed at bay. Until she went to bed that night, when the memories came back so that she had to take a sleeping pill from the small store she possessed.

It left her heavy-eyed and jaded next morning. Dane came home, iron-hard but rather drawn about the eyes and mouth, and smiled at her as though he was really pleased to see her. Dear God! she thought, trying to calm her throbbing nerves. She must be strong, or her life would indeed be the hell Ginny had predicted so graphically.

So when he said lazily, 'I've booked a table for us at the Mango Tree,' she shrugged and returned:

'Why, Dane?'

His eyes quizzed her. 'Because I feel like taking you out to dinner. Call it a reward for your efforts with the family.'

'I don't need a reward. That's my job.'

His glance hardened. 'Then because it's my whim.'

No doubt, she thought bitterly, saying as she moved away, 'Ah, but not mine. Thanks, Dane, but—no.'

Incredibly he smiled, catching her by the wrist and bringing it up so that the erratic beat of her pulse fluttered against his lips. 'But yes, sweet cousin. Or I'll come and put you in the car myself.'

The resolute note in his voice unnerved her and the touch of his mouth against her skin turned her bones to water, but she pulled away, replying pettishly, 'Don't be silly, Dane. I'm not one of your ladies, to be wooed into submission. Can it be true that you've been turned down so rarely you don't know a refusal when you see one?'

'What's that on your throat?'

For a moment she thought she was going to faint. Her other hand flew to the tell-tale mark, covering it protectively from the hot gold of his gaze.

'Nothing,' she lied, adding when his brows contracted in disbelief, 'I—I walked into a branch. It's nothing, Dane.' Her voice sharpened. 'Let me go please. If you want to take someone to dinner take Ginny. She's back.'

'Is she, indeed?' He said the words softly, almost without inflection, but the arrogant cast of his features hardened. Jerking her towards him, he bent his head to examine the scratch on her neck, after pulling her other hand away. 'Have you put anything on that?'

'Yes. It's all *right*, for heaven's sake!' Her voice was ragged with emotion and not every ounce of will power she possessed could prevent her from swaying very slightly towards him.

Instantly he held her by the shoulders, tilted her face so that he could see it, smiling.

'Then be ready at seven,' he said softly, and bent his head and kissed the mark, soft kisses along the length of it which fired her blood with an unbearable longing. Whirling, she ran, seeking safety in the refuge of her room and the very necessary dampening effect of a cold shower.

It was easy to say no. What was impossible was forcing Dane to accept her decision. She knew that if he had to he would make no bones about invading her bedroom and hauling her off, subduing with careless ease any efforts she might make to fight him. And she would get no help from Maurice.

A tiny kick of panic in her stomach heightened the excitement which had begun to invade her body. Was this how Dane planned to procure her agreement to marry him? Ride roughshod over her protests and refusals until her got her as far as the church and then rely on her dislike of making a scene to carry the day?

But she had only Ginny's horrible assertions to rely on for information that marriage was what he had in mind, she thought, ignoring the deep unease that instinct had aroused in her long before Ginny's reappearance on the scene.

And no one witnessing that horrible scene could call Ginny balanced or stable! She had behaved like a mad-woman, down to the final lightning-fast slash of her nail. But Renadi must have seen Dane leaving her bedroom the night of the Club ball, and with the Fijian's down-to-earth practicality had assumed that they were lovers.

How had Ginny known that, unless it was that Dane had told her, as he'd told her so much else? It was un-likely that any of the staff here gossiped. He must have seen Renadi on his way to his own room, Meredith, burning with a bitter humiliation, finally decided. So he had laughed with Ginny over the fact that his little cousin had fallen in love with him! Very well then, she would prove that she was well able to control her emotions where he was concerned.

Although the afternoons were hotter than she had ever experienced, the evenings were still cool enough to need a wrap. Choosing a long-sleeved dress of mulberry silk jersey with a low, draped bodice and a skirt that moulded her body lovingly in a swirl of material, she pulled her hair back in a style which was more severe than those she usually wore.

It made her look older, more sophisticated. Very carefully she made up, using a foundation to hide the shallow scratch and the too obvious play of colour Dane evoked, then slipped on a Victorian dress ring of rubies set in gold. Another of her grandmother's pieces, all now given into her keeping by Maurice.

As she surveyed herself in the mirror she was well satisfied with her appearance, except for the neckline of her dress. A frown creased her forehead as she looked; it was lower than normal and although it was perfectly decent she felt that the clinging material and the neckline combined to make it too revealing.

A quick search in the jewel box brought to light a necklace of tiny grains of gold welded together to form an intricate yet delicate web of metal. It was Eastern work, she remembered her grandfather telling her, and it lifted interest from the swell of her breasts. Exactly what she wanted.

A last spray of 'Miss Dior' perfume and she was ready; in complete armour, she thought wistfully. After dropping a kiss in the sleeping Mark's cheek she walked sedately towards the drawing room, shoulders straight, head held high.

'Just like Anne Boleyn on the way to the axe,' Dane told her disconcertingly when he met her at the door, the open appraisal in his glance bringing a sheen of angry colour to her cheekbones.

'You said it, not I.'

'Not that she was outstandingly beautiful, apparently. Perhaps Mary Queen of Scots?'

'Redheaded.'

Maurice watched them as they came across towards him, the thatch of his brows hiding his reactions.

'Hardly a fortunate lady,' Dane murmured lightly. 'Poor Mary! Too many lovers are not a good thing, even for a queen.'

If he had wanted to reinforce his power over her he had chosen exactly the right method. Beneath her make-up Meredith whitened, but her glance did not waver and she smiled at Maurice with the right amount of amusement.

'You look cross,' she said lightly.

'I am. Blasted body is starting to play me up. Pulled out all the stops tonight, didn't you?'

'That's just to show me that she's not intimidated,' the man beside her stated, infuriatingly accurate.

Maurice snorted. 'Warpaint—in my day no decent woman would have been seen with that amount of make-up on.'

'Now the decent and the frail look identical.' Dane smiled, his tawny eyes mocking her impotent anger.

Swiftly dropping to her knees beside the chair into which Maurice had sunk, she asked, 'Are you not well, Grandfather? Would you rather I stayed at home?'

'Don't fuss,' he ordered testily. 'Vasilau is better at coping with me than you'd ever be. Go on, get away off. I'm glad to be having a peaceful night for once.'

On an impulse Meredith kissed his cheek as she stood up. 'Goodnight, then. And if you frown like that you'll give yourself wrinkles.'

He laughed, 'Pert brat! Enjoy yourself.'

The Mango Tree was a nightclub attached to one of the big hotels at Nadi, unusual in that the food was Cordon Bleu standard and the band discreet. The more discerning of the locals patronised it, as well as an interesting cross-section of visitors. Because the prices were as high as the standards it was way beyond Peter King's purse; consequently Meredith looked around her with interest as they were shown to a table. From the waiter's respectful recognition of Dane it was clear that he was a regular. No doubt he had frequently escorted Ginny there, she thought waspishly, alarmed at the despair beyond jealousy which tied her in knots at this thought.

The decor was subdued. No fake Polynesian or Oriental touches here, just the best use of an enormous stone wall, orchids clinging to it like clusters of exotic insects, discreet lighting and superbly comfortable furniture. And unobtrusive air-conditioning.

'A drink?' Dane asked quietly.

It was no effort to shift her glance back to him. Light moved over his hair in a wave as he leaned back in the chair, emphasising the hawkish strength, the masculine beauty of his features.

In a voice suddenly husky she said, 'Yes, please. Sherry.'

'I'm glad you haven't acquired the cocktail habit,' he commented after the waiter had gone.

Perversely this annoyed her. 'Why? I've tried some, but I haven't found many I've liked.'

'They ruin your palate for a meal.'

'Really?' The sherry was dry, clear and crisp on her tongue. An excellent wine, she thought wryly, knowing that Dane was something of a connoisseur. Beneath the house lay a cellar, kept cool by the earth, where an enormous selection of wines waited patiently in the gloom. He always chose the wines for meals, marrying them with the food so that both blended to make a superb repast.

'Yes,' he said now, revealing his awareness of her unspoken challenge with a swift glinting smile, and proceeded to add fuel to her irritation by ordering a meal for her as if she had no will or desires of her own.

'Now banish that sullen expression and dance with me,' he ordered, taking her acquiescence for granted.

The floor was pocket handkerchief size, and there were many couples already on it, so any attempt at normal dancing was impossible. And this was certainly not the sort of company in which one danced in the abandoned modern fashion, Meredith thought, a tremor vitalising her body.

But Dane was equal to anything. Drawing her close, he put both hands on her waist. When, startled, she looked up he smiled, and said smoothly, 'If you put your hands on my shoulders you'll be less likely to lose them in this jam.'

It was like an embrace, her hands resting on the width of his shoulders, his relaxed yet purposeful against her narrow waist. Meredith's expression froze into complete blankness, so intent was she on keeping under control the incredible sensations his nearness was producing in her. Awareness prickled along her nerves, sensitised her skin so that she could feel the driving purpose within him and knew that it was directed at her. But when she was bumped from behind he gathered her closer, resting his cheek on her forehead in a gesture which had something of tenderness in it.

Just this once, she told common sense, relaxing the taut muscles so that she fitted more gracefully against him.

Instantly he stopped, saying with a derisive smile, 'It must almost be time for our meal to appear. Shall we go and wait for it?'

And that leaves me high and dry, Meredith thought confusedly, knowing that some of her frustration must be shadowed in her face but determined not to reveal just how this tortuous game of calculated advance and withdrawal affected her.

During the meal Dane was urbane, amusing in a dry manner, listening to her when she spoke with an interest which she was almost certain was not faked. He was excellent company, she thought, clever yet with a breadth of vision not often met, and under his influence she lost her wariness and spoke freely.

Several times he stood to speak to people who greeted him, introducing her as his cousin with a bland mockery which made her want to kick him. What on earth was he up to? she wondered; sometimes positively avuncular, at other times behaving as though he was bent on seduction. And in between charming the heart from her breast. Probably getting his kicks from her confusion; in the dim lighting, carefully contrived so that the food was revealed but the diners' faces in shadow, it was hard to gauge his expression. Which meant that he couldn't see hers either, although he was astute enough to be able to judge her reactions from the movements of her hands and head, as well as the tones of a voice she was trying to keep carefully neutral. Probably she was entirely predictable, she thought with gloomy desperation.

But oh, he was like a drug in her blood, stimulating her to animation, the like of which she had never before experienced. She felt as if she had champagne running through her veins although she had drunk little more than her usual glass with the meal; it wasn't until he drew her to her feet that she remembered to count the aperitif and the liqueur, for her head spun and she thought, horrified, I'm tight.

'No, you're not,' he said, reinforcing her conviction, for she must have spoken aloud. 'A trifle elevated, perhaps, but that will wear off. Dance with me once more and then I'll take you home.'

This time she relaxed against him as if she had the right, and his arm tightened; his hand roved sensually over the skin at the nape of her neck, weakening inhibitions already loosened by the potent combination of alcohol and his magnetism.

'Meredith,' he said softly into her ear, and when she lifted her head brushed her forehead with his lips.

An arrow of intolerable desire pierced her to the very centre of her being. For the first time she realised the full extent of the sensual servitude she was encouraging, but the flames in Dane's eyes seemed to leap up and engulf her, preventing any thought, any display of common sense. Swaying, she closed her eyes, not caring that her face must reveal everything she was experiencing.

'Don't go to sleep on me,' he said, hard mockery flicking like a whip.

Slowly her lashes lifted, met the cool amusement in his eyes with total bewilderment.

'What are you doing?' she breathed.

'Taking you home,' he returned, deliberately misunderstanding her.

Numbly she turned, walked with studied grace back to the table to pick up her bag. Women looked at Dane as they passed, some slyly appraising, some with open appreciation, assessing him both as man and lover. He was a taunting, calculating devil, she felt like telling them, able to undermine the most carefully erected defences with his controlled sexuality.

Somewhere at the back of one eye a flicker of pain pulled, settled into a regular throb.

At the door of the corridor leading to her room Dane said coolly, 'You looked tired out, my dear. Sleep in tomorrow morning.'

If I ever get to sleep. 'I'll do that,' she said tonelessly. 'Goodnight, Dane—and thank you.'

'Just one thing——' he said, turning her so that she faced him. His hand burnt like fire through the material of her gown, heavy on her arm.

'Don't——!' she exclaimed fiercely, the pain behind her eye increased so that she saw him haloed by a pulsing aura of light. 'No, Dane, I don't want you to kiss me.'

'Then I'm afraid you'll have to bear with me,' he said, 'because I very much want to kiss you.'

'I shall hate it!'

He laughed at that. 'Don't be such a dramatic little idiot! You'll enjoy it.'

His mouth was firm, devastating in his technical mastery. Meredith moaned softly, pain and ecstasy so mingled that she didn't know where one began and the other ended. After a moment he lifted his head, but only to kiss her eyelids shut. 'You're as white as the moon,' he stated softly, 'What is it?'

'You.'

'Nonsense. Tell me, Meredith.'

It was surrender of a sort, but she had no strength left to resist him. 'I've got a headache. I get them sometimes, but if I go to bed and sleep they go away.'

'Poor baby,' he mocked, a glimmer of tenderness in his voice. 'Too much excitement is bad for you.'

Before she could protest he had picked her up. It was bliss to rest her head against his arm, to allow him to take over. If her suspicions were correct she need only give in and her life would be as simple as this, all decisions made for her so that she need only be docile and efficient. No doubt the pleasure of keeping control of whatever money Maurice intended to leave her would compensate Dane for the fact that he believed her promiscuous. And she knew enough of him now to realise that he was more than confident of his powers of keeping her chained to him by ties she would never want to break. Golden chains forged by the senses, and steel ones made up of her fear of him.

For the first time, stripped of her self-possession by pain, she faced the fact that he frightened her. That ruthlessness she sensed in him struck at the basis of her confidence; she did not understand strength so disciplined that he could pass on to a business associate the woman he had intended to marry and contemplate another loveless relationship without qualms.

A shiver racked her as he put her on the bed. She could not marry him. Love could only bring happiness if it were reciprocated, and it was as useless to expect him to love her as it was to imagine snow in Fiji.

Dane must have had some acquaintance with headaches, for he did not put the light on, and after a moment left her. She had barely time to be surprised before he was back.

'Renadi is going to help you into bed,' he told her calmly. 'Have you tablets?'

'In the bathroom cabinet.' She pressed a hand to her forehead, saying in a muffled voice, 'I'm getting to make a habit of this.'

'Stress affects people in odd ways,' he returned.

After Meredith had taken the tablets Renadi helped her undress, murmuring gently and before long, drugged oblivion overtook her.

'What's this I hear about a headache?' Maurice's voice was scornful, as if she had failed some test he had set her.

'Migraine,' she said succinctly, feeling the blessed relief of freedom from pain.

He snorted. 'Too much to drink, more like.'

'Goodness, but you lot have nasty minds!' Delicately Meredith lifted a glass of pineapple juice to her lips, toasting him with an irony that won a half-smile in response. 'No, you'll have to acquit me of carousing. Ask Dane if you don't believe me.'

Odd that she could say his name without a tremor.

'Hmm. He left a message for you, by the way. He's going up the coast to see the manager of a Santa Gertrudis stud we own up there. He thought you might like to go with him.'

Meredith pretended to consider. 'No, I don't think so. I haven't seen much of Mark these last few days. I'd like to have a lazy day with him.'

'Take him with you,' her grandfather said shortly. 'It's only a couple of hours' drive on a good road. The Andersons have a young family.'

'But Dane might not want to.' She laughed, trying to infuse her voice with light raillery. 'Taking a two-year-old on a car-trip isn't all cakes and ale, you know.'

'Sometimes,' her grandfather pronounced, 'I wonder if you're deliberately obtuse. Dane is well aware of that fact, I can assure you. He's taking Mark, whether you go or no. Now go and get into something a little more suitable than those shorts.'

'No, I mustn't forget who I am,' she retorted bitterly, angered by the fact that in this household her wishes went for nothing. Pampered and cared for though she was, even treated with indulgence when she was obedient, both men saw her as a puppet, one more pawn in the gigantic game they played.

Fixing her with a frigid stare, Maurice said impatiently, 'If you don't like the system, Meredith, get out. Your mother thought life owed her a free lunch; in this world you get nothing without paying for it.'

'I don't mind paying,' she cried, 'but I hate being ordered around like—like a halfwit!'

'When you show a little sense we might stop.'

Half poised to run, she looked across at him, met the hardness of his stare without flinching. 'Indeed. And what might showing a little sense entail?'

'If you don't know I'm not going to point it out to you.'

'No, I'll bet not.' She walked away through the golden sunshine, for once blind to the cheeky antics of the red and grey bulbuls as they flew from tree to tree. God help her, for she could feel the wires of the hunter's noose tightening around her throat.

Maurice was right, the road was excellent. At any other time she would have thrilled to the views, the avenues of mango trees alongside the road, the enchanting children on their way to school dressed in identical uniforms of blue or pink or, incredibly in this country of dirt roads, white.

'How on earth do they keep clean?' she wondered aloud, waving delightedly at a group of adorable infants. 'Both Mark and his clothes are filthy ten minutes after he's put them on.'

Dane slanted a non-committal glance her way. 'Speaking as one who caused my mother's hair to go grey because of constant scrapes and subsequent dirt, I don't know,' he said. 'Both the Indians and the Fijians are extremely clean peoples.'

Nodding, Meredith turned to check Mark's well-being. Perched high in his safety chair, he could see exactly where he was going, yet was as protected in an accident as it was possible for him to be. Procured by Dane, it was another example of his thoughtfulness.

'Happy, my darling?'

He favoured her with his wide cheerful grin. 'Happy, Meddy?'

'Oh, yes. Very happy.'

Again she suffered that swift sideways glance. 'You don't exactly look happy,' Dane murmured. 'Do your migraines normally leave you heavy-eyed and sullen?'

He was being deliberately provocative, of course. 'Invariably,' she retorted firmly. 'By the way, I haven't thanked you for getting Renadi for me last night.'

'Think nothing of it. I was tempted to put you to bed myself, but I thought it might be less stressful if someone neutral did it.'

By keeping her eyes firmly fixed on to an Indian woman in a magenta sari Meredith hoped to hide the blush which covered her cheeks. 'You were right,' she said shortly. 'Dane, tell me about your parents.'

'My parents?' An odd inflection in his voice caught her attention. 'My father died when I was eight or so. I remember him as a periodic visitor who made my mother weep. He was an alcoholic.'

The level voice held no emotion, but Meredith's heart was wrung. Very vividly her imagination supplied the details which it was clear Dane had no intention of recalling for her. 'I'm sorry,' she said softly, afraid that he might consider her a probing busybody.

'It's a long time ago,' he returned with indifference. 'Maurice heard, of course, and stepped in. He and my mother had some right royal battles over my upbringing, but between them they hammered out a compromise and I grew up looking on this as my second home. My mother died five years ago. She married again and had years of happiness before her death. And that's my family history. How about yours?'

'I—I beg your pardon?'

The glance was very sharp this time, a rapier thrust at her self-confidence. 'I get the oddest notion that you've remained silent about large chunks of your life,' he observed, swinging the car off the main road on to one of the dirt tracks which turned inlands towards the distant purple peaks.

'You don't really expect me to spill out every detail of my life before I came here, do you?' she asked sharply, while a sliver of fear found its way into her consciousness.

'No, but you seem to have left out such a lot. Of course, you're never exactly forthcoming, are you? A very reserved lady.'

Attack, she thought painfully, with difficulty preventing herself from glancing at Mark. Aloud she asked, 'Well, what do you want to know?'

'The circumstances of Mark's conception interest me greatly,' he returned.

Shock, and the despair she had recognised before, held

her silent for a moment. Alongside the road the grass was high, dotted with large red cattle, vaguely oriental in appearance, who stared with bucolic interest at the car. A thick cloud of dust rose from the rear wheels. On the other side of the tiny home of a cane-grower nestled in a bower of pink and lilac bougainvillea. Far ahead the hills were covered with the dark green of pine forests. In spite of the air-conditioning it was very hot.

Wiping her palms on her handkerchief, Meredith said coldly, 'I've no intention of satisfying your curiosity.'

A narrow smile didn't soften his profile. 'And you think the less of me for probing such a delicate area? I happen to consider it rather important.'

'Why?' she demanded through stiff lips, not daring to look his way again in case the painful intensity of her emotions became apparent to him.

'Oh, certain things don't seem quite in character.'

The silence had a watchful waiting quality, which intimidated her. As if driven to it she blurted, 'Why did you take Don Poole on? It was you who organised it, wasn't it?'

'Yes,' he admitted without emotion. 'Fortunately he's turning out quite well. Philip Lamont says he has quite a future ahead of him.'

'Don't play games with me!' Her voice shook. With an effort she brought it under control, holding her hands so still in her lap that their rigidity must have revealed the tension which had her in its grip.

'Why not? You've played games with me ever since you arrived here.'

'If I have it's for good reason,' she muttered.

With icy control he said, 'Young Poole was hired because after the embrace I witnessed and your indecent haste to get to your *hure* I thought he might be needed as a husband.'

Feeling as though he had flayed her, Meredith refused to follow her body's instinctive desire to press back against the seat. So he still thought of her as promiscuous—perhaps after all he didn't know about Mark, and had merely been drawing a bow at a venture. Aloud she said stiffly, 'I see. Far-sighted, as usual. But you didn't know who I was, then.'

'I'd seen your name in the register,' he told her.

'I see,' she repeated, convinced now that if she allowed herself to be pitchforked into marriage with him she would deserve everything she got. He couldn't have made his contempt more plain. Far better to love at a distance than to be put through hell as his wife.

'I doubt if you do, but I'm afraid this fascinating conversation will have to finish. This is the place.'

## CHAPTER NINE

THE car swung on to a long driveway lined with rain-trees, passed a set of cattle yards and some sheds before leaving the main drive and winding up a hill that faced the distant sea.

Halfway up, in an arbour of lush green which contrasted with the golden rolling grasslands all about, was a house, very modern, very ranch style.

So were the Andersons. Meredith liked them immediately, enjoyed their irreverent attitude to life and the total lack of that sycophantic attitude she had sensed in the firm executives and their wives. Keith Anderson enjoyed his job, knew that he was good at it and with a splendid self-confidence got on with it, giving deference to no man. Not even Dane. Meredith found herself watching her cousin, and strangely was relieved to realise that he enjoyed Keith's frankness. It made him more approachable, she decided.

And Lois Anderson, though conscious of Dane's virile magnetism as all women were, was obviously very secure in her husband's love, secure enough to tease his boss gently. They had two children, an outgoing, bossy small girl who immediately took Mark under her wing and another a year or so old who spent all her waking time scuttling across the floor on her bottom, using one leg as a kind of paddle to propel herself around.

'It's the only way she knows,' Lois defended her off-spring cheerfully. 'And she gets around as fast as anyone, don't you, my poppet? No, don't smile at Dane, silly baby, he's being rude about your crawling. Dane, is there a female anywhere who can resist you?'

'Vast numbers,' he returned, unperturbed as the youngest Anderson pulled herself up against his knees. 'Meredith, for example, thinks I'm quite insufferable.'

His hostess's mischievous glance fastened on to Meredith's face. 'Well, I can understand that,' she said cryptically before returning to a subject she had raised before. 'Look, why don't you stay the night and go up to the mission? Meredith would love it, and don't tell me you haven't clothes, because I'll bet that you both have a hold-all in the car with spares. We never travel without them ourselves, and neither does anyone else with a toddler. Do stay, Dane.'

For a moment the tawny eyes searched Meredith's, then he shrugged slightly. 'Why not? As you say, Meredith has seen very little of Fiji yet. A trip to Rakiraki will give her a glimpse of the wetter areas.'

So it was arranged, and that night they had perhaps the most pleasant evening Meredith had spent since she had arrived in Fiji. Dane was always perfectly in command, of course, but with the Andersons he was relaxed, a teasing, witty, totally charming guest. And for once she could relax too, shrug off a few of the inhibitions that kept her aloof at her grandfather's home. Keith and Lois were interested in her, but showed none of the curiosity which her presence seemed to excite in everyone else, and when they retired after an evening of laughter and good conversation she was surprised to discover how late it was.

The two cars set off early next morning, almost before the sun had risen, sweeping along the silent roads towards the daybreak.

To the left glittered the dangerous shoals of the Bligh Water, the stretch of ocean which separated the two main islands of Fiji, dwarfing a tiny steamer picking its way towards Fiji's second largest island to the north.

'Can we see the other island from here?' Meredith

asked as the silence stretched between them.

'No. The road is too low. Somewhere out there is the rig. We're searching for oil. The Government hopes it might discover a field big enough to supply Fiji's needs, but no luck so far.'

'Dane, tell me about the Mission. Evidently it's something special, but I didn't have a chance to ask about it last night.'

'I think I'll let you discover it for yourself,' he said after a moment. 'Do you mind?'

'Why—no.' But she was surprised. However, she settled down to enjoy the scenery, admiring the tiny sugar railway which ran beside the road, the neat *bures* and yet more immaculate waving schoolchildren with their broad smiles. Dane, of course, was a splendid guide, pointing out landmarks, views and ancient fort sites including one Navutu Roek which had a replica standing a mile or so out to sea.

'Thi island is where the dead leave for their spiritual home,' he told her. 'I believe New Zealand has a similar legend, but there it's one of the northern capes.'

A little further on he pulled up beside a square grave on the side of the road. By now it was hot, and when the Andersons joined them they drank cold pineapple juice while Dane told them of the chief who was buried there, a cannibal who had, in his day, eaten a vast number of his fellow men. It was very still and peaceful; a plant with pink flowers grew up to the square stone box which had the Chief's name on it.

'Udre Udre,' Meredith pronounced, listening to the sound of doves in a tree. 'Charming man!'

'Well, things were different in those days.' Lois was tolerant. 'He was probably a kind husband and a doting father.'

A tot of about four marched along the road towards them, an enormous knife, almost a machete, casually carried across his shoulder. '*Bula*,' he greeted them enthusiastically.

There was a chorus of '*Bula*' back, before Dane said something in Fijian which made the little chap burst into laughter and scuttle on his way, chubby legs working hard in the thick gravel.

'They become independent early,' Dane said drily as he noticed Meredith's horrified gaze on the enormous knife. 'Ready to go now?'

Past the hotel at Rakiraki shaded by its huge banyan tree they swept on through a landscape greener and more lush than any Meredith had yet seen.

'Rice,' Dane pointed to where an Indian family swung knives in a field of grain by the sea. 'It's dry farmed here.'

The hills were closer to the coast now. For some miles the road ran alongside the sea, separated only by a rice field or mangroves, or a line of raintrees. There were many more trees, even growing up the steep volcanic hills; where the soil had been ploughed by slow teams of oxen it was a rich chocolate brown.

Then in a huge bay where coconut palms rustled about wooded capes and hills, a dirt road headed almost straight up a hill to level off in front of a stone church approached by an elegant set of steps.

'Novanibitu Mission,' Dane informed her laconically, handing her the scarf Lois had lent her to tie over her hair.

It was very quiet on the flat area before the church in spite of the school at the foot of the hill. No one seemed to be about, apart from a woman over by one of the buildings.

Quietly Meredith hushed Mark, awed by the deep peace she sensed here.

And the church literally took her breath away. Empty of pews, their place taken by beautifully woven mats with gay edgings, it led the eyes to the magnificent murals on the altar wall. Painted by a master, the Black Christ brooded over the church, majestic, enigmatic against the leaves of a mango tree. On the left were Fijians bearing offerings, a whale's tooth and folded *masi*, cloth beaten from the inner bark of the breadfruit tree, and a cleric. The other side had an Indian woman in a magnificent sari and another cleric, backgrounded by two oxen.

Two other paintings showed the young Christ working with his father in a carpenter's yard and Mary, interrupted by the angel of the Annunciation as she was making a mat.

'It is—like something out of a legend,' she said on a long breath. 'Who was the artist?'

'Jean Charlot.' It was Dane who spoke, softly yet with his usual authority so that she thought, of course he would know.

He and Lois took it in turns to tell her of the symbolism of the paintings and the circumstances of the murals' presence in this isolated spot. Mark leaned, silent and absorbed, against her legs, his wide gaze never leaving the paintings. After several minutes Keith took his two children outside; their voices could be heard on the soft air. Through the open door one could see straight out to the sea, framed by palms and trees.

On the way home, much later than they had estimated, she said abruptly, 'Thank you for taking me there.'

'My privilege.' In any other man the words would have been meaningless, but somehow Meredith thought that he really had considered it a privilege.

Sighing, she snuggled down into the seat.

The crackle of the car radio brought her awake again. With a yawn which almost split her face she sat up. The heat across her cheekbones was due more to the fact that she had been sleeping with her head on Dane's shoulder than the late afternoon sun which streamed in through the windows.

Dane was speaking into the handpiece, his voice strangely harsh. 'Yes,' A pause and then, 'We'll be there in half an hour. Tell him that.'

As he replaced the handpiece she asked urgently, 'What's happened?'

'Maurice has had another heart attack.' His voice was toneless. 'The doctor says there's not much hope. He's in Lautoka Hospital.'

The image of her grandfather's indomitable face and carriage seared her. 'Who was that?' she asked half under her breath.

'Vasilau. He seems to think we'd better get there as fast as we can.'

'I see.'

As if angered by her softly spoken answer he said savagely, 'Don't, for God's sake, pretend a sorrow I know damned well you don't feel!'

Shaken by the attack, Meredith retorted in a small hard voice, 'You really do despise me, don't you? You call me promiscuous, but I haven't noticed you keeping your hands to yourself. Apparently you can only be trusted near unsullied virgins! And you have the unmitigated gall to think you can sort out the sheep from the goats! For your information, you self-righteous hypocrite, I don't want to see Maurice dead. I may not love him, but I do respect him.' Fiercely she finished, 'I wouldn't even like to see you dead, and you I neither love nor respect.'

The frozen fire of his glance flicked across her tormented features. With a return to his normal self-possession he said coldly, 'I've no doubt you feel better for that little outburst. Now shut up and let me concentrate.'

Driving at speed in Fiji was made dangerous by the many pedestrians and animals on the road, but Dane handled the car like a professional, taking no risks yet keeping the car at well above the speed limit, so that it seemed only a few minutes before they were at the hospital.

A much needed few minutes. Meredith grabbed at her temper, feeling ashamed at her outburst. Hard and cold Dane might be, worthy of every epithet she had flung at him, but he loved Maurice, and it was grief which had made him cruel this time. She should have understood, instead of behaving like a bad-tempered child.

'He'll want to see Mark,' was all that Dane said to her as they went into the building.

He lay dominating the narrow hospital bed, his eyes fixed on the door with fierce purpose.

'About time,' he whispered harshly, ignoring everyone else but Dane. 'Get—rid of this lot.'

A few words from Dane drove everyone but Vasilau from the bedside.

'Good.' He spoke with difficulty, yet with such strength of will that it was useless to try to prevent him. 'Meredith . . .' he made two attempts to say her name, managed it on the second. 'Promise me . . . this.'

'Yes.'

He almost smiled, the fierce old eyes raking her face. 'Always find out . . . what, first. Marry Dane . . . now!'

'Grandfather——'

'I want . . . Mark . . . to have a father. Dane.' A greyness seemed to settle on to his skin. The harsh tired features contracted. '*Dane* . . .'

'She'll marry me,' Dane promised, his hand painful on her arm. 'Won't you, Meredith?'

Defeated, she nodded, said, 'Yes, Grandfather, I'll marry him, I promise. Now, try to rest.'

'*Now!*' Maurice said, more thickly. 'Vasilau . . .'

Incredibly, Vasilau ushered in a minister, a bewildered, middle-aged cleric who had obviously been summoned from his usual Saturday afternoon pursuits. The oddest sensation of dreaming assailed Meredith as she clutched at Dane's arm, aware of the sharp fierceness of the old man's glare on her face.

'Dane?' she whispered.

He was a million miles away, looking at a piece of paper Vasilau had handed to him.

'Yes, that's it,' he said, and took Mark from her arms, handing him to Vasilau. Those bronzed eyes were icy cold now, forbidding her to argue or question as he said gently, 'Darling, I know it's not the sort of wedding either of us want, but we can do this so that Maurice will be here.' No one could have known that the hands which grasped hers were like fetters, that he was daring her to make any objection with a cold ferocity which frightened her.

'Dane—I——' She drew in a sharp breath, her gaze bewildered. The skin of her throat moved as she swallowed convulsively. 'Yes,' she said, aware now that this had been inevitable ever since she had arrived in Fiji.

The ceremony was short, the ring a signet taken from Dane's finger; halfway through Mark woke and came to stand between them, his dark eyes large and wondering as they exchanged vows.

Afterwards everyone went out quietly and Maurice said, 'Couldn't do much . . . for Dinah. Weak, and stubborn with it. You'll . . . do. You and Mark. With Dane.'

Eyes fixed on the child, his lids drooped and he seemed to sleep. Afraid, exhausted yet deeply moved, Meredith felt tears prick beneath her lids. Indomitable to the last, the old eagle died as he had lived, imposing his will on those near him.

'Goodbye,' she whispered, unaware that she spoke. Dane's hand on her arm relaxed slightly; she turned, saw that his profile was as hard as stone.

'Get the doctor,' he ordered roughly.

'Too late,' said Vasilau.

Dane nodded, looking across the bed at the man who had cared for Maurice so well. 'I know, but get him just the same.'

Back at the house Meredith relinquished Mark to the very subdued Renadi, showered and changed into a dress. On her finger Dane's ring was heavy and too big. It had been warm when he had slipped it on, warm from the heat of his body. Suddenly shivering, she walked outside on to the veranda and sat in a cane chair in a small alcove surrounded by pots of splendid orchids. Their faint perfume floated across her nostrils, setting her nerves on edge.

When Dane appeared it was almost dark. 'Drink this,' he said abruptly, putting a glass into her hand.

A soft scrape revealed that he was pulling up a chair to sit beside her. She heard the faint creak of the cane as he settled into it.

'I don't think I want it,' she said numbly. 'Dane, is—was that a legal marriage?'

'Oh yes.' He sounded angry. 'Apparently Maurice got the licence some weeks ago. He had an idea that he might die. The venue had to be changed, that's all, but the circumstances made that easily done.' His glance at her downcast head was sharp. 'You should know Maurice better by now than to think that he'd leave anything to chance.' The bitterness in the deep tones made her shiver.

'We'll just have to have it annulled, then,' she said.

He laughed. 'And risk having him come back to haunt us? Not on your life! Why the shocked surprise? You must have known that he wanted us married.'

'And you?'

'Use your common sense,' he said derisively.

'As little as I, I suppose.' She sipped at the drink angered by his cold-blooded indifference. 'I knew as soon as you foisted Ginny off on to that company man what you had in mind. I despise you, Dane.'

'Drink up,' he ordered harshly. 'You're overwrought, and no wonder. I suppose it's not often that you find yourself outmanoeuvred. Forget it for the moment, will you! I've been in touch with Australia and by tomorrow midday I'll have a list of those who'll be coming to the funeral. The most important will stay here, of course; the rest will go into the guesthouse. Can you cope?'

'I'll have to, won't I?'

Her voice was desolate. Dane reached out and tipped her chin towards him so that his shrewd gaze could roam the pale exhaustion of her countenance. Astonishingly the burnished hardness of it softened as he noted the dark shadows under her eyes, the barely perceptible tremble of her underlip.

'Don't let his death weaken you,' he said almost gently, releasing her. 'You've style and spirit; he admired those qualities in you just as I do. We'll cope, Meredith.'

'With a loveless marriage?' She took a large gulp of the drink he had mixed for her, setting the glass down with a clunk on the glass table top. 'Dane, I don't want to be tied to you for the rest of my life.' And God forgive me the lie, she said voicelessly.

'I'm glad you realise that it's for life.'

'But there's no need——' Frustrated and stammering, she jumped to her feet. Exhaustion made her clumsy; the glass went flying, rolling across the verandah floor in a sparkle of spilt liquid. 'Oh, *look* what you made me do!' she cried childishly, unable to hide the tears which sprang to her eyes.

His soft laughter made her gasp with rage, but when he pulled her down on to his lap she didn't resist, betrayed by the swift response of her body.

'Calm down, darling,' he said, cruel amusement colouring his voice as he held her hands still in her lap. 'I don't want a weeping bride in my bed tonight.'

Cold terror stopped her breathing. 'What what do you mean?' she whispered.

'You heard.'

A tiny drum beat in her ears as her pulse rate accelerated unbearably. It was quite dark now, except for the subdued light spilling out from a room halfway down the verandah and the only birds singing were the doves in the big raintree beyond the garden.

Dane must have showered when he came home, for mingled with the characteristic scent of the orchids was the more astringent tang of aftershave. And another, tantalising, erotic, the clean male scent which emanated from his skin.

He moved slightly, pulling her into a more comfortable position, his body hard and muscular against hers, his hand keeping her still so that she was acutely aware of his strength.

'*No!*' she whispered, struggling to free herself.

'Oh, yes.' Effortlessly he held her against him, his free arm clamped around her waist. 'You're going to have to act as my wife, Meredith. It will be much easier for you if you are just that. I have no intention of sharing a bed with you and not asserting my rights.'

'We won't have to share a bed.'

She felt the muscles of his face move as he smiled. 'Don't be an idiot. Litia and Renadi are busy transferring your clothes to my room right now.'

'I can't,' she said frantically, trying to ignore the way his hand was cupping her breast. 'Dane—I *can't!*'

'You can and you will.' When she lifted her hot face pleadingly he kissed her, a teasing taunting kiss which further accelerated her pulse and rendered her silent. 'After all,' he said against her mouth, 'it's not the first time, is it?' I can understand that fear of the unknown might make you anxious. But you can't plead that, can you. Can you?' as she remained silent.

'No,' she said, her mind racing furiously. If she revealed that she was not Mark's mother he might have the marriage annulled and send her away, freed from a tie he had never wanted. At least he hadn't yet twitted her with his knowledge of her love for him.

Tears gathered in her eyes. What an incredible mess. If he felt anything other than passion for her he could not speak so lightly of her supposed experience.

'Don't sound so ashamed,' he said coolly. 'As you so frequently point out, I can hardly blame you for your experience when my own is not small.'

An unguarded movement betrayed her reaction to his words.

'Does the idea worry you? I hope I don't have to reassure you that there'll be no more. I've always felt that marriage is an excellent reason for faithfulness.'

The silence which followed was tense; beneath the calm mockery of his tone there was anger. Meredith thought she knew why. No doubt his coldly logical brain had pointed out all of the advantages of this marriage, but perhaps he had hoped to be initiating a virgin into the delights of sensual love. To be forced to marry her must be a blow to his pride. One that he should have come to terms with, she thought angrily.

'Aren't you going to threaten me?' she asked huskily. 'Demand that I remain faithful too?'

He laughed. 'No, I don't need to, sweet cousin. You needn't worry; I'll keep you so busy that you won't have time to be looking about for diversions.'

The note of lazy sensuality in his voice made her heart beat suffocatingly high in her breast, conjuring up as it did visions of nights spent in passionate felicity in his arms, captive to his dark masculinity.

'I *can't*!' She took him by surprise, leaping to her feet, but he stopped her before she had taken three steps by the simple expedient of grabbing her hair.

'Ouch!'

Her hands flew up to her maltreated head. Carelessly, roughly, he turned her, ignoring her kick at his shins with contemptuous amusement.

'Oh yes, you can, you little witch,' he muttered before kissing her with fierce concentration, crushing her mouth beneath his.

Meredith trembled, panicked by the ferocious intensity of his embrace. He was angry, but there was something else, something which made him cruel and implacable, determined to wrest submission from her.

'Open your mouth,' he muttered. 'Just what the hell do you think you're playing at?'

When she tried to tell him his tongue flicked between her lips, exploring, tantalising, savouring her in a kiss unlike anything she had ever experienced before. Desire was an ache in her breasts, a contraction in her stomach; once more she felt the sweet frustration of need.

'Kiss me,' he ordered harshly. 'Don't you know how to please a man?'

His breath was warm in her mouth, dangerously erotic. 'No,' she said, pulling back against the prison of his arms.

'Then it's about time you learned.' He picked her up and strode along the verandah with her held prisoner in his arms, his expression in the soft light grimly forbidding.

'Let me go!'

He grinned down at her, his glance lingering on the softness of her mouth. 'Calm down, Meredith.'

She should, of course, yell and struggle, force him to release her, but because she thought that her resistance amused him she remained sullenly tense in his arms. And of course, she had no foreknowledge of what he intended. Indeed, she expected him to dump her into a chair when he carried her through the parlour.

It was only when he turned into the corridor which led to his rooms that it occurred to her what he had in mind. And even then she could not credit it, for the door to his room was open and from it came Litia's voice, humming a Polynesian love tune.

'She, at least, has no illusions,' said Dane, eyeing her dilating eyes with derision.

'You wouldn't dare . . .'

But he would, she didn't need his taunting smile to tell her that, and when he deposited her on the bed she felt herself pale as he spoke to an openly laughing Litia in Fijian, telling her not to disturb them unless he rang.

'And now, madam wife . . .' he threatened, turning back to the enormous bed as he pulled his shirt over his head.

'Have you gone mad?' Meredith asked, terrified yet

unbearably excited by his blatant sensuality as he came towards her, a leaping flame heating the amber eyes.

'No. I want you, you've known that ever since you arrived here. I can see no reason to delay the inevitable.' Irony twisted his mouth as he watched her scramble up on to the pillow. He bent and clasped her ankle, pulling her forward into his arms.

'I haven't said goodnight to Mark,' she whispered.

'He was asleep when I came home.'

There was a note of amusement in the deep voice which emboldened her to lift her eyes. His gaze was unnerving, passion mixed with anger and that hidden something she recognised now as pain.

Of course, he grieved for Maurice.

'Kiss me,' he whispered deeply. 'Put your arms around me, Meredith. Be generous.'

Like an automaton, at the mercy of her love and the desire which was a vital component of it, she lifted her hands, shaping his face with a touch which was light yet devastatingly intimate. 'Dane,' she said, knowing now that she must tell him the truth. 'I . . .'

He laughed, angry laughter, and crushed the tumbling words to nothingness, reinforcing his physical domination without effort as he shifted position, bringing her to lie half under him.

'Love me,' he said, after minutes during which he taught her how voluptuous his mouth could be.

She could not speak, but he smiled at the expression beneath her half-closed lids. 'Not so difficult, is it?'

Full length beneath him she could feel the hard pressure of his thighs, the tension in his muscles as his desire flamed into a consuming fire. Against her will she found a matching need within her. When he removed her clothes she did not resist, although she flushed scarlet as his glittering gaze imposed possession on her body.

'You're beautiful,' he said huskily, kissing the hollows in her throat while one hand fondled her breast, calling into being an infinity of sensations. 'Beautiful.'

Beneath his mouth her skin bloomed. She looked down at the dark head against her breasts and arched convulsively against him, her hands pressing him to her in a gesture which was as revealing as it was sensual.

After that betrayal she lost all ability to think coherently in a limbo where the only realities were his hands
and his mouth and the scent and feel of his body as he
caressed and kissed her until at last they fused together and the aching tension exploded into a rapture
beyond belief.

'Open your eyes.'

Gasping, her hands clasped across his back, she looked
up at a Dane she had never known. Flushed skin taut
across the prominent bones; his eyes were like flames, all
enveloping, his mouth compressed by passion. Then the
rapture became anguish; she called out and became lost
in the incredible sensations which swamped her into oblivion.

## CHAPTER TEN

WHEN Dane pulled her across to lie with her head on his
chest she blushed, embarrassed by her wanton response to
his expert seduction.

'I think we'd better talk,' he said, tipping her head up
so that he could watch her face.

'About what?' Her eyes were fixed on to his face with
painful intensity, trying to read what lay behind the enigmatic mask which had replaced naked passion in his
face. Surely the rapture they had shared would enable
them to understand each other better.

'About the arrangements for Maurice's funeral.'

Hoping that her chagrin didn't show, she muttered,
'Oh. Well, what about them?'

His fingers tightened on her arm so that she winced
away, protesting, 'Dane! What on earth—?'

'Speak with a little more respect,' he said harshly, releasing her to swing off the bed. 'You told me that you didn't love him but that he'd won your respect. Show it, then.'

Bewildered by his withdrawal, she sat up, forgetful of her nakedness, unaware of anything but a cold anger that after such an earth-shaking experience he should shrug himself into a robe with his usual casual arrogance. It was as though he had relegated the pleasure and the ecstasy to some far corner of his life.

'Very well, then,' she said, her voice hardening. 'I'm ready to hear your orders.'

He turned, smiling narrowly. 'Leave it, Meredith. You can't behave like a wildcat in my arms one minute and try to pretend that you feel nothing for me the next.'

'I'm sure I shouldn't have to remind you that lust and liking needn't necessarily go together,' she retorted spiritedly. 'You've been an excellent teacher.'

He came back to sit beside her, keen-eyed, a mocking smile curving his mouth. Meredith couldn't look away, her glance held by the hard irony of his. 'It's too late,' he said softly, allowing his eyes to rest on her mouth, then drop to the rounded swell of her breasts and the slender line of thigh and leg. With one finger he traced a path from her throat to her navel, smiling when she flushed and dropped her lashes, driven by a swift pang of desire to realise that her need had become a fire in her blood. One that could end by consuming her completely.

Forcing herself to sound normal, she asked, 'What's too late?'

'For you to pretend that you're indifferent to me,' he murmured, his hand a path of flame on her skin.

'I should have known better than to expect that anything would change,' she retorted bitterly. A tremor shook her. It was impossible to ignore the tantalising movement of his hand as he touched each sensitive hollow. Her breath came swiftly through her lips; she couldn't bear the cynical appreciation of his glance any more, realising that he was deliberately showing her his mastery of the responses of her body.

'Damn you!' she exclaimed, folding her arms across her breasts in frustration. And even that was no good, for he laughed and pinned her wrists together above her head, forcing her back against the pillows so that she lay exposed to the insolent ravishment of his gaze.

'By all means.' He dropped a kiss on the smooth length of her throat. 'But perhaps I'd better spell out to you exactly what I expect of you.'

Disillusion twisted her mouth into a wry grimace, but she congratulated herself on the normality of her voice when she answered, 'And then I'll tell you what I expect of you.'

'You've got guts,' he told her drily, the cold appreciation replaced by something like amusement. 'But in this game I hold the winning hand, Meredith.'

And the tone of his voice, as well as the knowledgeable glance at her body, told her that one of the cards in that hand was the physical response he won so easily from her. And the other was the fact that he knew of her love for him.

With nothing more than cool authority in his voice he continued, 'There's no reason why we shouldn't make a success of this, after all. Sexually we're well suited; not even you could deny that, however much you'd like to. You show a charming lack of modesty and restraint, and I've never made any attempt to hide the fact that I find you desirable.'

'Arrogant devil!' she choked, made miserably aware of how great a defeat she had just suffered.

Dane shrugged, releasing her as if she bored him. 'Have it your own way. Would you prefer a romantic fraud? Shall I vow eternal love and promise you the moon, make a lying mask to hide the reality of the situation because you're too blinded by wishful thinking to accept the truth? Would I possess an adoring wife if I told you that I loved you?'

'No!' The anger and pain she felt brought colour back into her face, gave her the energy to slide from the bed and make her way across to where Litia had left an armful of clothes over the back of a chair. With trembling fingers she extracted a towelling shift usually worn to cover her bikini and pulled it down over her head, conscious of the fact that Dane watched her with that hard cynicism she hated. Her heart wept, but she forced herself to appear calm, as calm as he. Later she would mourn for lost innocence, the naïvety which had led her to hope, for such a short time, that their shared ecstasy had somehow wiped the slate clean of all that had gone before.

How stupid! Dane was a sophisticated, ruthless man with a wide experience of women. And although she had pleased him with her ardour there must have been over the years, many other occasions when he had felt that intolerable pleasure in a woman's arms.

No doubt it was a change to have to stage a seduction, she thought wearily, staring down at hands which had delighted in the knotted muscles of his back as he had invaded her body. But her response had obviously pleased him. It had been, after all, one hurdle out of the way. Now he could count out the other steps he considered necessary for a good marriage, and then if she made a mistake or stumbled it would be her fault. Clever, calculating Dane! Heartless Dane! Why, oh, why did I have to love you? she thought.

'Looking for blood?'

The lazy words startled her. Her glance flew from her hands to meet his watchful mocking gaze.

'What?'

'Blood.' He shrugged his shoulder free from the robe, revealing to her horrified glance scratches which testified to the primitive abandon of her passion.

'Dear God!' she whispered, appalled.

He laughed, and rose, and came to stand in front of her, that ironic, worldly smile emphasising the cruel line of his mouth. 'I suppose I should be honoured. Clearly you haven't reacted like that before, but I've known right from the start that we strike sparks from each other. Got over your pique?'

'Yes,' she said quietly, lashes lowered to hide her thoughts, the wilful curve of her lips tightening into a straight line.

'Right. Then come and sit down, and we'll talk with as little emotion as we can manage.'

Taking her hand, he drew her to an area of the big room where chairs waited beneath a magnificent landscape in oils, its hard vivid colours and bold forms symbolising the savage fecundity of the tropics.

'You'd better have something to drink,' he said when she was seated, and poured her out a long drink using the small refrigerator built into the wall along with a sink and glass storage.

'All modern conveniences,' she commented, after the first cautious sip. 'This is lovely. What is it?'

'A Mai Tai.' He grinned. 'And don't let anyone ply you with them. Delicious they are, but with a kick like a mule.'

'Just what I need.'

His smile changed quality, became taunting. 'That bad, was it? Never mind, Meredith, within a few weeks you'll be more accustomed to my lovemaking.'

This open avowal of further intimacy brought a sparkle of anger to Meredith's glance, but she said nothing.

After a moment's keen stare he resumed, 'However, there's no need to go into that now. Tomorrow the family and the firm will begin descending on us.'

'Like a pack of ravening wolves,' she said, half under her breath.

'I've no doubt the family will be interested in the contents of Maurice's will, but as far as the firm is concerned everything was decided several years ago. Maurice didn't suffer from delusions of immortality.'

As the deep voice continued Meredith found herself wondering whether it was grief at Maurice's death or merely the aftermath of passion which set such a distance between them. Was this chilly remoteness to be an accepted part of their life together?

Repelled, yet aware that it was stupid to ignore what he said, she began to concentrate, head bent over her drink to avoid the ache which came when her eyes rested on that cold profile.

He spoke incisively, paying her the compliment of addressing her as an equal. After a while she managed to push the pain and embarrassment to the back of her mind. Then, so suddenly that she was unaware of any tiredness, she slept.

When she awoke it was with a jolt of astonishment at hearing Dane's low voice beside her. He was speaking into the telephone, and as recollection surged back she knew who was at the other end.

'. . . and thank you,' he said smoothly into the darkness. A short silence, and then, without emotion, 'There's no reason why you should absent yourself from anything unless you want to, my dear. You needn't worry about how Meredith will receive you. Nothing has changed.'

Another silence while the tinny little voice at the other end quacked, then he said with crisp courtesy, 'No such thing! Neither she nor I are given to absurd fancies. I can promise you that she'll treat you with all her usual courtesy.' After a few moments spent listening he said goodbye and hung up.

'You speak for yourself,' said Meredith, yawning, one hand on the faint pink mark that Ginny's nail had left on her skin. 'You don't know me well enough to be able to be that confident about my reactions.'

He laughed, and slid beneath the sheets. 'No?'

Evidently he slept naked; the warmth of his body against hers revealed that, but he had also put her to bed without a nightgown, so that when his lips found her shoulder there was nothing to prevent his hand from sliding from her breast to her thigh and then beneath her hips. He pulled her hard against him, laughing at her indignant gasp when she realised that he was ready to subject her to another merciless onslaught of the senses.

'I didn't mean——' She stopped as a traitorous heat made itself felt in her blood. His mouth incited her to yield to its temptation when he kissed the soft roundness of her breasts. A groan forced its way through her lips. Slowly, as if in a dream, she touched his shoulders, the desire within her growing at the smooth strength of the muscles beneath his skin.

His mouth continued on its enticement. When his lips

closed on her breast she gasped and arched herself against him, unable to control the fiery passion he evoked so swiftly within her. But even as she responded she drew back. Into her mind sprang a nagging doubt. Was it Ginny's voice that had awoken his desire?

He laughed again, cruelly this time, and said softly, 'Care to take back what you said? The little bit about my not being able to judge your reactions.'

'*Devil!*' she spat, her fury driving her to close her teeth on the skin of his shoulder.

'She-cat!' Dane rolled over on to his back, lifted himself on an elbow and held her throat, the long fingers tight enough to let her feel their strength, yet not so tight that they bruised. 'Don't be provocative if you don't intend to take the consequences.' he said thinly, his features in the dim light strong-boned and harsh.

'I didn't intend to be provocative,' she protested, every nerve aching with frustration as he released her.

He moved away so that there was no contact and rolled over on to his back. 'I don't believe you.' He spoke quietly, each word cold and clear. 'Women are born with the knowledge. Learn to control that tongue of yours, Meredith, or I'll control it for you.'

'You enjoy threatening me, don't you,' she stated, only just managing to banish misery from her voice.

'I don't enjoy threatening anyone.' Apparently he wasn't tired, for he joined his hands behind his head, turning his face slightly towards her so that he could see the faint outline of her profile against the window. 'For some reason you like to think of me as an ogre, intent on making your life as uncomfortable as possible, but all I've ever done was to try to protect those I feel an obligation to.'

'Maurice and Ginny.'

'Maurice and Ginny,' he agreed. 'Maurice was an old man, and the fact that Mark was his only male descendant was extremely important to him. I may have been a little harsh with you when first we met, but in the circumstances I think my attitude was justified. Part of it, at least, was caused by the fact that I wanted you.'

To hear the level voice so coldbloodedly discussing his desire for her made her catch her breath. What kind of man was this who could lead her to the heights of physical ecstasy, then behave as though she was his office girl? It was impossible that she should love such a man. Yet her pride lay in the dust. She loved him more than life.

'And Ginny?'

'If you hadn't arrived I would have married her.'

Well, she had wanted to know, but the knowledge was dearly bought. A shaft of anguish kept her motionless, as if by lying without movement she could will it away. Eventually it ebbed, to be replaced by an anger so deep and cold that she was sure she could never be warmed again. Slowly she unclenched her hands, hugging herself for protection. Beneath her arms the beat of her heart was slow, painful in her breast.

'I see,' she said at last, her voice a thread of sound. 'Do you think I should apologise to her? Perhaps we could get together some time and exchange views on how you rate as a lover.'

'Jealous, Meredith?'

She reacted to the sardonic amusement of his tone with scathing scorn. 'Why should I be jealous? I'm the one with the wedding ring; I can afford to be generous.'

'I hope so.'

There was a long silence during which she fought a battle with jealousy, feeling it tear at her emotions with clutching greedy fingers. Perhaps it was then that she moved from being a girl to a woman's estate. Raw with pain, she forced herself to face the bitter facts, and with acceptance came a kind of peace. She had fallen in love with a Dane who existed only in her imagination. Deceived by charisma and physical presence and her own youthful inexperience, she had tumbled into infatuation, hoping that somehow he would learn to love her in return.

How very naïve! It was unlikely that Dane knew the meaning of love; certainly he understood the convolutions of sexual attraction, but he had proved by his attitude tonight that he felt nothing for her except desire and his respect for what he termed her Fowler characteristics, her brain and organisational ability.

Very well then, she thought, trying to rise above jealousy and hurt pride and the aching anguish that his attitude inflicted on her. He was right, of course; plenty of successful marriages had started with less going for them than that. If she worked at it no doubt she could make herself necessary to him. Would it be worth the price, the constant need for self-control, the dampening down of the love she felt?

There was really no alternative. Dane would not let her go with Mark, and Mark needed a father figure in his life. And if she had to sacrifice romantic illusions for the practical reality—well, wouldn't that have happened sooner or later anyway? It was very few lovers who could share a rapturous certainty all the days of their lives. Most marriages settled down into prosaic matter-of-factness after a few years, so she had heard.

At least life with Dane wouldn't be dull!

But there was something she had to know before she finally relinquished her hopes and dreams.

'Were you and Ginny lovers?' she asked quietly.

'No. I'm sorry to have to disappoint you, but I'm not really at all like the picture you've manufactured of me. I'm not inexperienced, but I don't go around bedding every woman I feel desire for.'

'Like Ginny?'

As soon as she spoke she knew that she should have kept quiet. This probing into an area of his life that was no concern of hers revealed her jealousy and the dreadful hollow vulnerability her love forced on her.

Sure enough, he sighed. 'Like Ginny,' he agreed drily, and snaked an arm beneath her shoulders. 'Feeling insecure?' he muttered as he turned her to face him. 'Will this convince you that Ginny is the past and that I'm only interested in the present—and the future?'

This time he was more gentle, wooing her with voice and hands and mouth, superbly in control, while she lost her head completely and responded with an ardour she had never thought to experience, a shuddering, desperate, wanton creature completely at the mercy of her hunger for oblivion in ecstasy. For some strange reason she wept when it was all over, the tears forcing themselves beneath her lids to fall on to his chest.

'Oh, Meredith,' sighed Dane, half mockingly. 'What on earth am I going to do with you? Here, you're making me damp. Use this.'

When she had mopped up he smiled, and kissed her. 'Something on your mind?'

She nearly told him then, impelled by her need to wipe the slate clean. Fortunately she thought of Ginny, who hadn't hesitated to ring him on his wedding night, Ginny whom he desired, and the impulse turned cold within her.

'No,' she said huskily. 'Why should I have? Everything is fine, isn't it, just as Maurice wanted. You get an efficient wife and Mark has parents who love him and Fowlers is safe for another generation at least. Why should I complain? I get a rich husband who turns me on every time I come within ten feet of him——' He laughed, but there was little amusement in the sound, though he said, 'Could be awkward, but I'm glad you are not too shy to tell me how you feel.'

'And how do you feel?'

She got the answer she deserved. 'Tired,' he said mockingly. 'It's been a long day.'

'Goodnight, then.'

There was a quality of tenderness in the way he kissed her and held her until sleep claimed her, a tenderness which was the only thing she had to console her in the days that followed.

Meredith found herself inundated by Fowlers, besieged by them, almost swamped by Fowlers of all different ages and shapes and heights and degrees of wealth, all inordinately interested in this latest addition to the family. They felicitated her and the feminine half kissed Dane and the male half claimed kisses from her; they made a fuss of Mark and ate and drank and talked and talked and talked, until she thought she would go mad with their avid, relentless curiosity. Not that it was malicious; they obviously felt that Maurice had done the right thing in organising this marriage, and if they didn't they were too much in awe of Dane to say anything. Even Meredith on occasion could summon up a look of cool hauteur which precluded any indiscreet questions. But she felt tired, and each night she fell into bed beside her husband and slept instantly, to wake with a jolt every morning to another day of exhausting, weakening activity.

And at the back of her mind always the niggling thought that the passion he had woken to life within her had made her so responsive, so forward that he had not known he was the first man to have taken what she had offered so ardently.

But at least he showed no signs of being interested in Ginny. And he had plenty of opportunity for Ginny and Mrs Moore were there all the time. Just as if nothing had happened, as if Ginny was still an honoured guest, acting as a kind of secondary hostess, and maddeningly discreet about the whole business. As if she had never spat poison at Meredith and lost control so horrifyingly.

The scratch had faded by now, but every time she saw Ginny Meredith felt it, hot and stinging down her throat.

'You're doing wonders,' Mrs Philip Lamont murmured encouragingly, after Maurice's funeral. 'But you could do with a rest, I think.'

'Does it show?' Meredith liked Mary Lamont and was disposed to trust her, even though she seemed to think that the merest smidgen of Fowler blood elevated one above the common herd.

'Only to those who like you,' the older woman answered soothingly. 'I notice that Dane is keeping a close eye on you.'

Making sure that she didn't need help, but Meredith wasn't going to tell her that.

'He's very possessive,' Mrs Lamont mused. 'He always has been, of course. I think it must be a necessary part of that buccaneer personality. It was a pity that Maurice's death precipitated things. I had hoped that you would have a nice long courtship. I could see that Dane was smitten, of course, but you didn't seem at all certain of your feelings towards him, then.'

'When?' Meredith was somewhat bewildered by this gentle monologue.

'When we were here last, of course. There was a young man mentioned . . .'

'Peter King.' Guilty because she had allowed Peter to drift out of her life without any explanations, Meredith found her eyes drawn to where Dane stood, tall and tough, overshadowing every other man in the big drawing room. He was talking to the local chief, a big, immensely dignified man in a superbly tailored *sulu* suit; with them was an Indian businessman who had been with his wife to dinner several times. They spoke quietly, seriously. Three men very much in command.

Everything was going extremely well. The drinks and food were circulating under Vasilau's capable eyes, the talk was appropriately subdued but intent. It was quite clear that no one but Dane grieved for Maurice.

The thought was so intolerably sad to Meredith that she blinked away strange tears, compressing her mouth to hide a quiver of pain. Poor Maurice, so rich, so powerful, and yet leaving nothing behind of any worth, unless it was Dane's affection. He had put his firm before his family, and he truly reaped what he'd sown.

But he had made sure of her welfare. The next day she discovered that she and Mark were the beneficiaries of a trust which would see them with an income far in excess of their needs. And Ginny had been right. The trustee, of course, was Dane. Everything else, the house, the paintings, the antiques, was left to him, except for the jewellery which had been Meredith's grandmother's and which was now legally hers.

'Very suitable,' she said drily to Dane in their room after everyone else had retired for the night. 'Did you know about it?'

He nodded. 'Yes. We discussed it.'

And then he'd discussed it with Ginny. Meredith watched as he poured out a small whisky. It was unusual for him to drink at this hour of the night; he was normally abstemious, but he was obviously under some strain. He looked as tired as she felt, the tanned skin drawn, the small lines about his eyes suddenly clear. As he stared into the liquid his mouth was harsh as though he subjected himself to a severe discipline. She felt a sudden wave of compassion. He had loved Maurice in his own way, loved him enough to give up his plans to marry Ginny to take on the cousin he despised with her supposedly illegitimate son.

Before she had time to think and change her mind she walked over and kissed his cheek. 'You miss him, don't you?'

He was very still, then he smiled and drained the glass. 'God, yes, I miss him. Isn't it fortunate for me that he organised our marriage? The ideal way to take my mind from my grief.'

'Is that how you see me?'

His lips curled into a caustic smile as he turned her, pulling her back against him. When he bent to kiss the spot where her neck joined her shoulder his breath was warm across her skin, disturbing her careful calm.

'What else are you?' he asked cruelly, his lips arousing shivery sensations deep within her. 'Certainly not a loving wife. You resent the fact that I can arouse you. You forced me to force you . . .'

His hands moved from her waist to shape her breasts, burning through the thin material of her wrap.

'You reduce everything to its most basic level,' she said huskily, feeling the tense rigidity of his body as he turned her to face him. 'And you know that you didn't have to force me—I wanted you as much as you wanted me.'

He was kissing her face slowly, tasting her, it seemed, exploring the lines and planes with a deliberation which maddened her. Glancing up, she saw that his eyes were closed. He looked tired, almost vulnerable.

'And what on earth is going to happen to us?' she whispered, lifting her arms to hold him across the shoulders, her voice betraying her doubts and fears.

'You're going to help me forget my grief,' he whispered

raggedly. 'When you're in my arms I can think of nothing but you, and what you do to me. I don't care what happens to us. I want the oblivion only you can give me.'

'Oh, Dane,' she breathed, tempted to tell him of her love and held back only by the knowledge that if she did she would be his possession, body and soul, from then on.

His eyes flew open as he dealt with her momentary hesitation by picking her up and tossing her on to the big bed. 'Oh, Meredith,' he mocked, staring at her with a merciless intensity which seared her. 'Don't look so frightened! You seemed to want me to make love to you a moment ago. It's too late to think better of it, as I'm sure you're aware.'

'Not like this,' she stammered, realising that her hesitation had been misread and that he was angry with her.

'Like this—and any way I want,' he said, sitting on the side of the bed, his hands remorseless as they pulled her wrap open. 'What's the matter—don't you want me now?'

She bit her lip, angered by the jeering note in his voice but afraid too, for he had never looked so implacable.

'I want you to make love to me,' she said, her glance soft with appeal. 'Not—take me, as though—as though . . .'

'As though you're a woman I've bought for the night?' He smiled without humour. 'Well, I have bought you, Meredith; the difference is that my purchase is for a lifetime. Maurice and I talked things over fairly early on in the piece and he made sure that I realised that if I didn't marry you the trusteeship would be left elsewhere. And as your trust owns a considerable number of shares in the firm it would have been a damned nuisance to me to have someone else in control of them.'

'Why are you telling me this?' Her voice was a mere thread of sound. He had dealt her a body blow, the kind that scars for life. She was cold, as cold as ice, and his hands on her were intolerable, but she couldn't move to push him away.

'So that you don't get any romantic ideas,' he said

harshly, ridding her of the wrap by peeling it from her and tossing it on to the floor on the other side of the bed. 'I'm no romantic hero, Meredith, thinking the world well lost for love, and don't you forget it. Whatever you feel for me is going to be based on truth, on cold hard fact, not on the mushy imaginings of a brain which can't discern between desire and love.' The hard gold of his eyes ravished the slim length of her body, insolently appraising. 'Why so stricken? You aren't a sentimental schoolgirl any longer, my darling. You've slept with at least one other man, borne his child, and coped with tragedy and a completely new life style. You run this house as though you were born to it, you have guts and intelligence and style, and between us we whip up a storm. Are you still hankering for a declaration of eternal love?'

'*No!*'

'Perhaps you feel that it's not polite to make love without it?' He laughed, but his eyes were piercing, stripping through the protective layers she had erected. A moment more and he would know.

'Shut up,' she muttered, and pulled him down, lifting a mouth that was hot and trembling to his as she used the power of her sexuality to divert him.

'Do you want me?' He spoke against her lips, refusing to accept what she offered him.

'Yes, damn you, yes!'

'Did your first lover tell you that he loved you?'

By now she was almost sobbing with frustration and anger. A high flush covered her skin as she turned her head, but Dane put a hand on each side of her face, holding it so that she could not move.

'Tell me,' he demanded. 'What was his name, Meredith? Where was Mark conceived? In the back seat of a car? Or in some wood? On your living room sofa, perhaps? How——'

'Will you *stop* it!' Her skin felt dyed scarlet from her forehead to the end of her toes. 'Leave me alone!' she gasped, held in the scalding ferocity of his gaze like a rabbit mesmerised by a snake.

A slow smile touched his lips. 'You hate it when I speak of your first lover, don't you? Why, Meredith?'

'Dane—please——'

'Look at me when you speak to me!'

But she kept her eyes tight shut, terrified that he would discover her secret, and after a moment he said harshly, 'Oh, for God's sake stop looking so terrified! I'm not going to rape you.'

When he stood up she felt cold, and shivered, opening her eyes to see him walk towards the door. 'Where are you going?' she asked.

'To do some work.'

Astonished, she waited until he had closed the door behind him before hurrying into her nightgown and sliding down between the sheets.

The clock chimed two before Dane came back in; she lay very still, breathing carefully, but he took no notice of her, removing his clothes in the dressing room before he got into bed. He had moved quietly but with no great care, as if he didn't care whether he woke her or not.

## CHAPTER ELEVEN

'You know, you've got thinner!' Sarah surveyed her companion with speculative eyes. 'I hope it's not the climate, because the wet season hasn't even started yet! And that's when things get sticky—and I mean sticky.'

Meredith forced a smile, refusing to meet Sarah's glance. 'No, it's not the climate. Both Mark and I love it.'

'Then what is it?'

Shrugging, she answered, 'Oh, just everything, I suppose. Maurice's death was traumatic, and then there was the inundation of relatives and Fowlers people. I guess I'm just tired.'

Sarah brushed coarse white sand from her legs as she sat up. They were in the deep shade of a *vai-vai* tree, beyond them the morning sun glittered and sparkled on the sea. All around was the soft hush of the wind in the palms, soothing, a little mournful.

Mark was building a sandcastle, his expression rapt as he patted the coral grains into shape. It was very peaceful, the only reminder that they were on an island of other people, the clouds of smoke from the Lautoka sugar mill billowing up to the horizon.

'Not to mention getting married,' Sarah remarked.

Meredith smiled, aware that her companion was delicately probing. 'Well, yes, although I knew that that was on the agenda,' she said lightly. 'We hadn't planned on being married so soon, but when Maurice was fretting it seemed the logical thing to do.'

'Well, it was a terrific surprise for all of us,' Sarah told her frankly, 'except for Peter, of all people! He was a bit green, but he said he'd always thought that Dane was keen on you. I suppose being keen on you himself sharpened up his perceptions.'

Meredith nodded, and murmured agreement, but said, 'I hope he wasn't too upset. I didn't mean to hurt him.'

'Lord, no!' Her companion was bracing. 'He always knew there was no hope. I mean, let's face it, you are a Fowler and your grandfather was loaded and Dane is absolutely swoonworthy! Add to that the fact that you're super looking and loaded with style, and you can see that Pete was content to worship from afar. As a matter of fact, he's rather fallen for a pretty girl whose father is a bank manager in Suva. She's a nice thing and her father is infinitely more approachable than Mr Fowler.'

This was a joke, so Meredith laughed, her conscience eased within her. The thought of Peter had given her some bad moments.

'We'd better get back,' she said reluctantly, glancing at her watch. 'It will be lunchtime soon.'

'O.K.,' Sarah grinned. 'I suppose you're still at the "can't-bear-to-be-parted" stage. What's it like being married, Meredith?'

She meant 'What's it like being married to Dane Fowler?' It was just as well that Meredith was bending over to pick up the big rug, or even Sarah, who was not noted for her perspicacity, might have seen that something was wrong.

As it was, her voice was oddly muffled. 'Wonderful.'

'Well, naturally.' Sarah laughed. 'But it must be difficult to get used to sharing everything. I've often wondered how things feel after the first rapture dies.'

'You didn't give us long,' Meredith observed wryly, packing the glasses and flasks back into the refrigerated bin.

Sarah laughed again. 'Whoops! Pete always says I only open my mouth to put my foot in it.'

With any luck she would never know just how right she had been, Meredith thought as the car bumped gently over the dirt road. Except that there hadn't been any rapture at all, merely those hours after their incredible wedding when he had made her realise her full potential as a woman. Since then—nothing! Long nights spent in the big bed with only the sound of his breathing to while away the hours. During the daytime he preserved a courteous, distant attitude towards her which hurt more than his anger.

Ginny Moore had been right: he had married her to get control of those shares. No doubt in his own good time he would demand a child from her, but in the meantime he was making sure that she realised just how little she meant to him.

A refined kind of torture, and she knew she was going to break under it if it continued for much longer. How Dane must hate this marriage they had been forced into, to be so aloof when he suspected her love for him. But then she had always known of the darkness which lay hidden beneath that polished surface.

Damn Maurice, who hadn't been content to die without playing God one more time. Sometimes in the long watches of the night Meredith thought she would die of hunger and need, but pride and the fear of humiliation kept her from stretching out a hand to him. She would not be able to bear it if he rebuffed her, or made some cutting caustic remark as he took her.

'We're running a bit late,' Sarah commented as the car

rejoined the sealed main road. 'I'll just drop you off and sneak away. I've got to finish my packing.'

Meredith nodded. Sarah was off to New Zealand tomorrow, back to university and the pleasant uncomplicated life she led there.

'We'll see you at Christmas?'

'Oh yes, I'll be back. It will be as hot as hell and wet, but I like it. Will you be here?'

'We haven't discussed going anywhere else.'

Strangely enough her companion looked surprised. 'Oh, from the way Ginny Moore was talking I thought you were going to spend Christmas in Sydney.'

Meredith bit back a sharp retort. 'Perhaps she is,' she said evenly, 'but I don't know about us.'

Her companion nodded, uneasily aware that she had once more said the wrong thing. 'Yes, I suppose so,' she returned vaguely. 'Oh, get that damned cow off the road!'

The tense little moment passed, but although Meredith chatted cheerfully enough her brain was fretting over the implications of Sarah's ingenuous comment. So Ginny was still hanging in there, taking it on herself to talk about their affairs. What hurt was the fact that she must have Dane's tacit approval; Meredith could not imagine that even Ginny would take it on herself to discuss their affairs without Dane's knowledge.

A red anger misted her sight. How dared they make arrangements behind her back, treat her as if she was a child! A retarded one at that. If Dane really thought that he could keep a wife and a girl-friend in harness he was going to have his mind changed for him. She was not a Fowler for nothing. Unconsciously her chin lifted. She was sick of this—this humiliating state of being a wife and yet no wife. Dane had shown her what her heritage could be, and if he thought that she could be kept in subjection to his whims he had not yet learned exactly what manner of person she was.

'You look very fierce,' Sarah observed as the car swept up the drive. 'Anything wrong?'

'Good heavens, no. I was planning a dinner menu,

that's all. I'll miss you, Sarah.'

A smile of pleasure widened the other girl's mouth. 'I'll miss you, too. You're an interesting person, Meredith. Quite demure-looking, and yet you have a kind of steely strength that is impressive.'

'You make me sound like Wonder Woman!'

They shared giggles.

'Nonsense,' Sarah said bracingly. 'It was a compliment. Actually, you and Dane match each other. He needs someone as strong as he is. I used to think he should marry a sweetly charming girl, but I think someone like that would bore him to screaming point.'

If only she knew! Feeling a hundred or so years older, Meredith said goodbye, wished Sarah luck in her exams, and took a sleepy Mark up into the coolness of the hall where Renadi met them and bore him off.

A murmur of voices drew Meredith into the drawing room. And there was Ginny, locked in Dane's arms, her hands either side of his face as she said, 'Oh, Dane! Why——'

Meredith had to repress a strong urge to pick up a jade statuette and hit that dark sleek head with enough force to kill her.

Instead she said coldly, 'That happens to be my husband you've festooned yourself around.'

And when Ginny dropped her hands and turned, so that Meredith could see the gloating triumph in her eyes, she continued, 'I think you should be a little more careful. What if I'd been one of the servants?'

It was an old joke, but one Ginny hadn't heard, for her mouth dropped open and she looked foolish, and yes, scandalised! For the first time Meredith let her eyes drift to Dane's face. He was coolly amused; there was no lipstick on his face, so apparently they hadn't spent long in each other's arms.

'You'll excuse me, I'm sure, if I suggest that you're distinctly *de trop*,' Meredith added, addressing Ginny with cold sarcasm. 'I'll ring Vasilau to take you back.'

'Oh, but Dane is.' Ginny put her hand on his wrist and infused a note of false commiseration in her voice. 'My dear, you mustn't get things wrong. Dane was merely comforting me—I've had some bad news.'

'It must be a day for bad news,' Meredith said with sombre emphasis, furious with Ginny, even more angry with Dane who would have kissed Ginny had they not been interrupted. Her anger made her pale beneath her tan, but there was a glitter in her eyes which transformed them to a turbulent darkness and her mouth set firmly above her stubborn chin.

'Meredith, you must remember that Dane and I are—old friends.'

The delicate innuendo made Meredith even angrier. 'And he and I are newlyweds,' she said calmly, holding on to her control. 'Both you and he should perhaps know that I don't share. Anything.'

He was watching her, ignoring Ginny, the burnished glance heavy with assessment. Any other man would have shown some sort of embarrassment, caught by his wife about to kiss another woman, but he was capable of outfacing anything. He stood, and she could feel his interest and something else, something she could not discern.

He spoke then, the deep voice without expression. 'A true Fowler characteristic,' he observed, and she knew that that something else was an anger which matched, perhaps overtopped hers. 'But nobody is asking you to share anything. Ginny's mother is ill.'

'Then shouldn't Ginny be home caring for her?'

'Why, you little——'

Ginny's voice was lost in Dane's sharp command for her to be silent. Arms folded as if only that way she could protect herself from them, Meredith stood fearlessly, her eyes fixed on the cruel lines of Dane's mouth. Deep within her she knew that she was suffering a hurt more grievous than any other she had ever experienced, but for the moment the wonderful anger blanked it out.

'That's enough!' he said, almost indifferently, yet with such a note in his voice that Ginny was silent, a high flush blotching her cheekbones. She looked hard and much older, her emotions running out of control. It was clear that things were not going her way and she was finding it hard to cope.

'I'll take you back,' he said to her now, his expression cold. The tawny blaze of his glance flicked across to Meredith and focussed for one disturbing moment on the pulse which jumped in her throat. 'You'd better say goodbye, as Ginny and her mother are going back to Australia.'

'I thought Mrs Moore was sick.'

'She is,' Ginny spat. 'She's going back for tests.' As if to underline her hold on Dane she turned and smiled, those long fingers tightening on his wrist. 'Thank you, darling, for arranging everything.'

Sick despair whitened Meredith's skin, but her pride held her head high as she said quietly, 'I'm sorry about your mother.'

'Thank you.' It seemed that Ginny had regained her confidence as Meredith's had ebbed away, for she smiled now, continuing smoothly, 'I don't suppose you know how I feel. My mother is very precious to me. She's sacrificed a lot for me over the years to see that I was protected from harmful influences. I used to think she was too old-fashioned and rigid in her ideas, but circumstances have made me realise how wise she was.' She waited, smiling as Meredith's pallor increased. Satisfied that the hit had gone home, she turned to Dane. 'I'm ready to go now, my dear. I'll write when we reach Sydney. I'm sure Meredith will allow me that small gesture.'

Oh, she was clever, and Meredith was sick of fighting her. How could she have hoped to win when Dane was so obviously on the other side?

But it took Dane to rub it in. 'Meredith doesn't vet my mail,' he said smoothly, a smile twisting his lips. 'And I'd like to hear how your mother is.'

'Well, that's that, then.' Ginny purred, satisfaction rendering her voice smug. 'Goodbye, Meredith.'

'Goodbye.'

But the torment wasn't over. As if to impress his ownership of her firmly on her mind, Dane came across and kissed her, his mouth hard against the surprised softness of hers. 'I'll be back in half an hour,' he said grimly.

Well, she was damned if she was going to be the meek little wife being firmly put in her place. 'Certainly,' she said politely. 'I won't be here, however.'

'Why?'

She lifted her brows in mock surprise. 'I'm helping Sarah pack. She's going back on the morning plane to-morrow.'

'Leave it,' he ordered, and when her chin came up he smiled. 'Or I'll come and get you.'

'Go to hell!'

He laughed and brushed her mouth with his lips in a kiss which was as unkind as a blow. 'I'll see you in half an hour, sweet cousin.'

Well, that had wiped the smile off Ginny's face, she thought as the door closed behind them. And hers, too.

Fortunately Mark wanted her to supervise his lunch; after he had given her a sticky hug and been led off to bed she had a shower and put on another dress, a floor-length butterfly affair she had bought in one of the local shops. It was a soft graceful thing with great floating sleeves in a clear blue lightened by a white hibiscus border around the hem. Cool and suitable, it didn't need anything underneath it but the barest of necessities.

The days were continuing to heat up, an indication of just how hot it would become over Christmas, when the poincianas were scarlet umbrellas and the raintrees tinted the hills with pink and the rain came down to bless the islands.

Was Dane intending to go to Sydney then? Well, Meredith thought with a mutinous jaw, he could go if he wished. She and Mark would stay here. And if it was the last thing she did she would prevent Ginny Moore from ever returning to this house.

Dane's arrival back was the signal for every nerve to tighten, but she refused to hurry. Indeed, when he came into the room she was spraying herself with perfume.

He shot a swift appraising glance at his wife's remote profile. 'Do you want a drink before lunch?'

'Lime juice will be lovely, thank you.'

The refrigerator door closed with a soft slam. She heard the tinkle of ice cubes as she put on a pair of lapis lazuli earrings the exact colour of her dress. Then the light in the mirror was blocked as he came up behind her, big and dark and still angry.

'Stop sulking and drink this.'

'I am not sulking,' she told him politely, refusing to turn because he was too near and he had no intention of moving away.

His glance in the mirror taunted, 'Then just what are you doing?'

'I'm angry.'

He was standing so close that she felt the smooth fabric of his shirt move when he shrugged. 'At least it's something,' he said crisply. 'I was wondering how long that cold façade was going to last.'

Astonished, Meredith turned, and immediately wished she hadn't. With a narrow smile he set the glass down on the dressing table and caught her across the shoulders in a grip she knew she couldn't break.

'What façade?' she demanded, determined not to reveal how much his nearness affected her.

'The one you've hidden behind ever since we were married.'

Her teeth caught on her lip for a moment, then she said curtly, 'You were the one who assumed the mask. I've just followed suit.'

'Well, there's something to be said for kissing Ginny,' Dane said calmly, his glance holding her pinned. 'It brought you out of hiding.'

The back of her throat ached. 'Don't try it too often,' she said grittily, 'or I just might lose my temper and kill one or both of you. I meant what I said, Dane. I won't share.'

'I'm not asking you to.'

'It looks very much as though you want to have your cake and eat it too.'

He smiled in irony. 'Will you believe me if I said I wasn't kissing her?'

'I know you weren't,' she said coldly. 'No lipstick. But if I hadn't come in what would have happened?'

'Nothing.' He smiled again at the look of disbelief she flashed upwards. 'You see, it was when she heard you that she stepped forward and arranged herself in such an artistic manner against me.'

'Adam's excuse,' she said scornfully. 'It wasn't me, it was the woman! Why would she do that?'

'To cause trouble.'

For a moment Meredith didn't think she had heard aright. Hardly daring to breathe, she fixed her eyes on the brown column of his neck while her brain raced into top gear.

After a moment she said carefully, 'I think I'll have that drink.'

Releasing her, Dane said, 'Bring it over here and have it in comfort.'

When she had sat down he stood gazing at her with cool deliberation, obviously waiting for her to speak.

Twice she opened her mouth to ask; the third time she managed to say huskily, 'Why should she want to cause trouble?'

'Probably because I'd just told her that if she so much as hinted to a single soul that Mark was your child I'd sue her for slander.'

It took Meredith some seconds to absorb this.

He continued drily, 'I'd already told her that I'd had the records checked before you ever set foot on Fiji and that I could prove that Mark was your brother.'

For a moment Meredith thought she was going to faint. Pulling herself together after the room had stopped turning, she gratefully sipped some of the lime juice before asking thinly, 'If you knew, why were you so horrible to me?'

'Don Poole.'

'I see,' she sighed. 'But why, Dane? That first day you hated me then, and it was more than the fact that you didn't want any blots on the Fowler escutcheon.'

He set his tumbler down, looked at her with a wry smile which belied the dark intensity of his glance. 'I've told you why. I wanted you.'

She shook her head. 'That's not good enough. There must be other women you've wanted; I'll bet you didn't call them names like wanton and—and—slut.' Her voice trembled.

'You want your pound of flesh, don't you?' he said, and moved across and hauled her to her feet, his hands savage against the soft skin of her shoulder 'O.K., take it. I didn't realise it at the time, but I'd fallen in love with you. Like that—the whole way. I saw you in the dining room on Hibiscus Island and went across to the register to see who you were. I wasn't very surprised when I saw your name; it seemed predestined. Then . . .' His mouth straightened into a hard, thin line. 'Then I saw you run into the *bure* with Don Poole, after he'd kissed you, and I could have killed you both. So easily.'

Of course she didn't believe what he was saying. 'You can't fall in love—just like that!'

'No? That's what I told myself, especially when it was obvious that nothing so shattering had happened to you. You settled in and trailed around with young King, happy as a lark; the only thing I had to console me was the fact that you disliked Ginny.'

His grip on her shoulders had relaxed into a sensuous caress across the skin exposed by the wide neckline of her dress. Much as she enjoyed it she could not allow him to continue until she knew exactly what he meant. 'I thought you were in love with her,' she said.

Dane bestowed a mocking glance on her.

'Well,' she hedged, 'I thought you wanted to marry her. She told me——'

'She told you what?'

It was difficult to meet the sudden flash in his eyes. 'That you would marry me because you wanted the disposition of my shares. You told me that too, so I thought you and she must have discussed it. As well as the fact that I'd told you Mark was mine. And——' she stopped precipitately, flushing and looking away.

'And . . .?'

Her tongue seemed to cleave to the roof of her mouth,

but she went on slowly, 'She said you knew that I—that I'd fallen in love with you.'

'When did she tell you all this?' His voice was harsh, taut with self-discipline, and his hands had stilled.

'The day before you came home from the Philippines. You noticed the mark on my neck.'

'She put that there?' The words were clipped, savage. She nodded, a little afraid at the raw fury which blazed up into his eye 'I thought you'd guessed.'

'No. I thought Mark had done it and you were protecting him.' He began to swear softly, continuing until she put her hand across his lips. Then he kissed the palm, his mouth warm against the soft skin; Meredith felt a bubble of excitement expand within her, and slid her hand up to rest against the side of his face.

'I don't know why,' she whispered, 'but I do love you. It would have taken more than a deathbed to force me to marry a man I didn't love.'

His eyes were sombre. 'I believe you.'

'No, you don't. Why? What must I do to make you believe me?'

He kissed her lips gently, and then forcefully, purging himself of hurt and anger. 'You didn't love me enough to tell me the truth about Mark, however much I taunted you. I asked you about it several times, but each time you refused to trust me. You made me so angry.'

So that was it! 'I wish I had,' she murmured. 'But I was so confused. I thought you and Maurice might take him away from me. And after we were married I felt I was punishing you for going about things in such a cold-blooded fashion! I hoped it would hurt you to think that there'd been another man before you.'

His arm tightened unbearably, bringing a gasp to her lips. Distressed, she looked up, met a glance as hot as the sun realised for the first time just how much she affected this man who was her husband.

'You're hurting,' she whispered.

'Good. I'd like to break you, but I'd be hurting myself too much.' His hand moved swiftly, pulling down the long zip at the back of her dress. 'You frighten me,' he muttered. 'You know exactly how to hit me for the maximum effect. Dear God, the nights I've spent wanting you—Meredith, I love you, and this time I want some co-operation. You're no longer a frightened virgin.'

The dress whispered to the floor leaving her naked except for her sandals and the flimsy briefs she wore. Instinctively her hands flew to cover her breasts. She stepped backwards, tripped over the folds of material and would have fallen had Dane not caught her.

'Don't run away,' he breathed, and set her on her feet again. Bewildered, she watched as he knelt and took her sandals off.

'At my feet, Dane?' she asked, her voice very low.

He looked up, eyes gleaming, sliding possessive hands the length of her legs to come to rest on her hips, kissing the hollow of her navel. His tongue was seductive, exciting every nerve-end throughout her body. 'Would you like me to be at your feet?'

'No.' She stooped and pulled him up so that they stood together. 'I like you—I love you, like this.'

Her kiss was openly erotic, promising all that she had withheld on their wedding night. Against her hands his heart thundered; without moving her mouth Meredith teased the buttons of his shirt free and slid her hands across his back, pressing herself against him, revelling in the need that his body revealed.

'Witch,' he groaned, picking her up and carrying her across to the bed.

'Brute!'

He laughed against the young tautness of her breasts and showed her how little she knew of love, expertly reducing her to a state of abject passion that made her whisper his name against the smooth skin of his shoulder, begging him to take her and release the frustration which had kept her awake night after long night.

'Tell me you love me,' she whispered, as he moved to cover her body with his.

'I love you.' For a moment he was motionless, then he pressed her on to the bed muttering, 'And I need you, Meredith, I need your love and your laughter and your kindness. I've loved you for ever, it seems.'

'And I love you.' As sensations exploded deep within her she gave herself up to the powerful magic of his love-making, her passion meeting and joining with his to carry them both to an ecstasy she had never imagined. His arms were cruel, his body possessed of a fierce energy which fed on her surrender, demanding a response equal to his hunger.

Freed from the tensions of their first lovemaking, Meredith found in herself a wild sensuality and an instinctive knowledge of what best pleased him, so that after their hunger for each other had climaxed in a crescendo of desire she was exhausted, her hands splayed across his back in a grip which only slowly relaxed.

'Now do you believe me?' she asked quietly, turning her head so that she could see his profile.

'Yes.' He smiled, and kissed her, and moved so that he was beside her on the bed. 'I have to believe you, otherwise I think I'd go crazy.'

'Dane!'

'Darling, I've know right from the start that I couldn't expect you to feel as deeply as I do. You're so young. I've lived long enough to know the difference between love and infatuation, but you haven't. You had a hell of a lot of growing up to do. That's partly why I made no attempts to rid you of your misconceptions.'

Meredith was puzzled, and a little afraid of his dismissal of her avowal of love. 'Which misconceptions?'

'Ginny, for one. I told you I'd intended to marry her. Well, it was true as far as that went.' His finger pushed aside a tress of pale hair from her cheek, gentle yet firm. 'Maurice had been suggesting marriage for some years, and I owed him some peace of mind before he died. Ginny seemed ideal. I have never loved her, but I'd be a liar if I said that I hadn't wanted her. I didn't care much, one way or the other. I suppose I've always had a grave suspicion of love matches; my parents were not exactly a good advertisement. Nor yours, if you're honest.' He smiled, and kissed her. 'And Ginny is intelligent and witty and restful, you must admit.'

Meredith would have admitted anything now. She couldn't even summon up any dislike for the woman.

When she told him so he laughed and taunted softly, 'Amazing how a few simple words can sweeten your temper, my darling. Well, all of that went by the board when I saw you, but I didn't know whether that untouched air was a fake—whether the little incident I'd happened on at Hibiscus was an innocent goodnight kiss or the prelude to sex. You insisted Mark was yours; I knew why, but the fact that you'd not borne him didn't mean that you were innocent. You wouldn't confide in me. So I was as curt as possible with you and I watched you like a hawk, trying to discover the truth. I hoped that a little pain might speed up the maturing process.'

'I hated you,' she said with sombre intensity. 'You despised me and I despised myself when you kissed me that first time and the whole world sort of exploded around me.'

'Yes, that taught me a lot too. But not enough.'

Something made her ask, 'If I had had an affair with Don, what would you have done, Dane?'

'Nothing.' The tanned shoulders shrugged. 'Oh, the thought of it made me see red, but I'm not entirely chauvinistic. There have been women in my life; why should I expect virginal purity when I can't offer it?' His smile was twisted, sardonic, as his possessiveness made itself apparent. 'When I heard you and Poole talking about your relationship I could have sung several Te Deums in praise. I won't deny that I'm glad that I'm the first.'

The kiss was deep, seeking, but before it could lead to what they both wanted she put her finger across his lips, whispering, 'No, let's get all the explanations over first, darling. How on earth did Ginny know so much? I realise that she was just guessing about Mark, if you already knew he's my brother. But the rest—the will, and about Renadi seeing you come from my room after the ball.'

'What was that?'

She told him, and he reacted angrily, a warning glitter in his eyes. 'God, she really tried, didn't she?' he said viciously. 'She must have sensed how you affected me right from the start, to be so accurate in her assessment of the situation. I forgot how astute she is.'

There was a silence, then Dane turned, the fury dying in his face to be replaced by a wry acceptance. 'I've never discussed you—or our affairs—with her. I had no idea that what you felt for me was love. I only wish I'd known. As for Renadi—well, her sister is Ginny's house-girl. She wouldn't consider it gossip to tell her, and I've no doubt that's where Ginny got that bit of news. I didn't even know! The Trust—well, I suppose she drew a bow at a venture and, damn her, hit the bullseye.'

Incredibly enough it seemed that he was appealing for her belief. Meredith didn't hesitate. Tracing the strong bones of his face, she said, 'I should have guessed, I suppose. I knew she hated me. If I'd been a little more mature I might have realised why. But she made it seem so logical, and of course I had no idea how you felt about me.'

'She knew,' Dane agreed. 'As I said, she's an astute woman. She knew I didn't feel anything much for her, but both she and Maurice realised that my reaction to you was pretty volcanic. She must have decided to make as much mischief as she could in the hope that she'd cause an unbridgeable rift.'

'I wish I'd told you about Mark,' she said wistfully, only now realising how he must have wanted her trust.

'I can understand why you didn't.' He spoke grimly, tenderness gone as he thought of the woman who had so nearly wrecked their love. 'My God, what a bitch! You must have thought me a complete swine.'

Meredith's smile was openly adoring, her eyes very soft and warm. 'I did, but I loved you. So much!'

He looked shaken, the tawny eyes firing into desire once more as he took in the slim delight of her body. 'If you could love someone who could behave the way you thought I had, then, dearest heart, I don't deserve you. I had to marry you, and then I had to take you in case you wanted an annulment after Maurice's death, but you'll never know how afraid I was that I'd spoiled everything for us. I vowed I wouldn't make love to you again until you showed me you wanted it.'

'I thought you'd satisfied your curiosity about me and

didn't want me any more.'

The gleaming lights in his eyes turned into flames, devouring her. 'Baby,' he taunted through lips only a fraction of an inch away from hers. 'I'll never have enough of you, never satisfy my curiosity. We're a pair, you and I, halves of the same whole. I knew that after a day or so; Maurice saw it, so, damn her, did Ginny. Even Mark couples us together in his mind. It was foreordained that you should come here and turn my life upside down.'

His hand lingered on her breast, sending a thousand thrills through her. Before he could kiss her she asked, 'Do you mind?'

'No. I love you—without you life has no meaning beyond a daily grind, to acquire money and power. You're the reason that I was born.'

'Ah, God,' she breathed, shaken to the core by this admission of his need. 'I love you, Dane, so much.'

As their bodies expressed their innermost yearnings she spared a thought for Maurice, who had loved his wife and died happily, expecting that Dane and she would share a similar love, for her mother, who had feared that Fiji would mean pain and disillusionment, for Mark, who would now have the inestimable good fortune to grow up in a household where love reigned.

Then Dane's mouth came down on hers, and as the South Seas prepared for the afternoon siesta she forgot all else but that voyage of the senses which was an outward expression of the love they bore each other. Safe in that love, the future held no fears for them.

# Harlequin Presents...

The books that let you escape into the wonderful world of romance! Trips to exotic places...interesting plots...meeting memorable people... the excitement of love....These are integral parts of Harlequin Presents— the heartwarming novels read by women everywhere.

Many early issues are now available. Choose from this great selection!

# Choose from this great selection of exciting Harlequin Presents editions

# Relive a great romance...
# with Harlequin Presents
## Complete and mail this coupon today!

## Harlequin Reader Service

In U.S.A.
MPO Box 707
Niagara Falls, N.Y. 14302

In Canada
649 Ontario St.
Stratford, Ontario, N5A 6W2

Please send me the following Harlequin Presents novels. I am enclosing my check or money order for $1.50 for each novel ordered, plus 59¢ to cover postage and handling.

| | | |
|---|---|---|
| ☐ 99 | ☐ 103 | ☐ 109 |
| ☐ 100 | ☐ 106 | ☐ 110 |
| ☐ 101 | ☐ 107 | ☐ 111 |
| ☐ 102 | ☐ 108 | ☐ 112 |

Number of novels checked @ $1.50 each =     $_____

N.Y. and Ariz. residents add appropriate sales tax.     $_____

Postage and handling     $_____.59

TOTAL   $_____

I enclose _____
(Please send check or money order. We cannot be responsible for cash sent through the mail.)

Prices subject to change without notice.

NAME _____
(Please Print)

ADDRESS _____

CITY _____

STATE/PROV. _____

ZIP/POSTAL CODE _____

**Offer expires January 31, 1982**

105563170